I0741487

COMPETITIVE INSTINCTS

RALEIGH DAVIS

Copyright © 2018 by Raleigh Davis

All rights reserved.

No part of this book may be reproduced in any form or by any electronic or mechanical means, including information storage and retrieval systems, without written permission from the author, except for the use of brief quotations in a book review.

CHAPTER 1

She's invaded my territory.

Doc sitting at a workstation in our secure facility isn't exactly an invasion though. It's technically not my territory for starters—it's owned by Bastard Capital. I'm one of six Bastards, all partners and founders of the firm, but I'm the one who uses this facility the most, so I consider it mine.

My second thought is... Well, it's not really a thought. It's a tightening of my entire body, a shift from *let's get some work done* to *she's FUCKING here, pay attention!* Really intense, yeah, but not super coherent, at least not enough to get called a thought.

She peers over the extra-large monitor at me, her purple hair appearing first. She's streaked it with lilac and gray, and it should look like a wig, but she makes it look like she was born with it.

Then come her bold brows set above her deep amber eyes. She's wearing heavy black glasses that a funky librarian would love.

Then her pert nose—the only part of her face that can be called sweet—and her lush mouth. Her mouth is so sensual it makes me think of hours-long kisses every single time I see it.

One brow is cocked skeptically, and her mouth echoes that sentiment. Ramona Blythe, PhD, is not impressed with me, but then she never has been.

I'm not bragging when I say I'm a genius. It's like saying that my hair is brown or my eyes are blue; it's just true. In fact, I'm a supergenius, which makes me a pretty big deal in the tech world where everyone gets called a plain old genius on the regular. But I'm a step beyond all those other guys. Again, not bragging, just speaking some truth.

Except Doc is one of the few—the *only*—people not impressed by my big brain. Every time we meet, she has to make it clear how little she thinks of me. And of course, since I'm an idiot when it comes to her, it turns me on every time.

"Hey." That's the only greeting she gives as she disappears back behind her monitor.

"Hey." I dump my stuff at a workstation where I can have a clear view of her. "What are you working on?"

"Stuff." She doesn't look away from the monitor. "January said I could use the servers here."

January is Doc's boss and the girlfriend of Mark, another Bastard.

"I know that." My fingers fly over the keyboard as I log in to my own workstation. "I asked what you were working on. You know, making conversation."

I know she loves chatting because she does it with everyone. I'm the only one who gets her pissy side. I guess I should feel blessed.

"Like I said, stuff." She hits a key with a flourish, probably sending something off to the servers to run. It feels like a triumphal keystroke. "What about you?"

Okay, so she doesn't want to tell me. Which is fair, because I don't want to tell her what I'm working on.

"Stuff," I say as I pull up my code. I launch the program, then pull up my web browser and log in to the Go forums.

Go is a game invented in ancient China, thousands of

years old with deceptively simple rules. More complicated than chess, Go is a meditation and a game all in one, and it's supposedly uncrackable by a computer.

There are two players—white and black—and one board, nineteen squares by nineteen squares. All you can do is place a single piece on a square corner with each turn, and the only goal is to capture and control territory on the board. Very simple stuff.

But, like life, things get complicated on the Go board very quickly. So complicated that even a computer can't follow the human leaps of intuition needed to play Go at the highest level.

Chess is a different story. Deep Blue beat Kasparov at chess by brute forcing the calculations. It was basically a really fucking big calculator. Deep Blue can't play Go, because it can't think. Not like a human can.

I can play Go because I *can* think. But… I'm pretty sure I'm smart enough to design a computer program that can think too—artificial intelligence, AI, aka the holy grail of the tech world.

Developing a thinking machine requires that I give it things to learn though. If I want my AI to play Go, I need to give it some human brains to practice on. So me and my AI are going to play some Go tonight and see if we can learn anything.

"Stuff," Doc echoes contemptuously. "I would've thought you'd be gaming."

I am, but she means something like a first-person shooter. Quick, dependent on well-honed reflexes, and not exactly meditative. "Nope. Just some work on something I'm testing."

Anyone else would look up from their console, ask me what I'm doing. I'm Finn Braden—whatever I'm working on has to be interesting, perhaps even world changing.

Doc doesn't even act like she heard what I said.

Fine. Whatever. I didn't come here to chat. I came here to test my AI.

There're several people in the Go forum, but none of them are at my level. Shit. I can't let my AI loose on some beginners. It'll whip all their asses without learning anything that will improve its performance. My machine doesn't understand nuance or being a graceful winner.

I guess I can play my AI, but it's kind of like jerking off—perfectly fine in a pinch, but my dick already knows all my signature moves. There's no surprise factor.

Okay, I'm totally pouting right now, and Doc is going to bust my balls when she catches me doing it—although that's an intriguing picture, Doc and my balls—but I wanted a challenge tonight. And I'm not going to get one.

Then a window pops up, announcing that QuikSilver has entered the forum.

Oh hell yes. I resist the urge to pump my fist. QuikSilver is my nemesis, my archenemy. They're exactly at my level, a consummate shit talker, and they have what I'd call a chaotic style. No, not chaotic—like a split personality. They'll be going along, playing beautifully, but a little too stodgy to be really great, then suddenly a switch will flip. Then comes some brilliant, crazy moves that I never saw coming. The very opposite of stodgy.

I want my AI not just to play Go—I want it to be able to predict what the other player will do, to watch their playing style and get into their head. I want it not only to think like a human but read its opponent like a human.

It's ambitious, but nobody ever accused me of setting my sights low. I'm a genius. So yeah, my computer program should be a genius too.

QuikSilver is the perfect person to test my AI on. I've never set my AI on them—it wasn't ready for a player of their level until now.

I rub my hands together, sneaking a quick look at Doc.

She's so focused on her monitor I'm surprised it doesn't catch fire. Her lips are parted, gleaming, and I swear I can feel her breathing from all the way across this room.

Thank God my AI will be playing instead of me, because I can't think for shit after seeing that.

I shake it off and focus back on my own work. I send a request to start a game with QuikSilver, which is immediately accepted. And then we're off.

I play the first game all on my own without running the AI. Yeah, I'll probably lose, but whatever. Mostly I want to get myself into the right headspace but also reacquaint myself with my opponent. People can't hide themselves when they're playing Go—their personalities are mirrored in each strategy, every move.

I've been told my style is someone who thinks too quickly and ponders too little, relying on flashes of insight to muscle my way through the game rather than thinking through a long strategy.

I'd say that's fair.

QuikSilver is definitely a long-term strategist. They're sly, the kind of person who likes to hide poisoned darts within an innocent-looking scaffold. There're no traps that I can see in this first game, but we're both getting warmed up.

Across from me, Doc keeps typing away, but her expression has taken on a new focus, like she's battling with her code. It's a damn sexy look on her. I mean, most of her looks are damn sexy, but this one is especially so.

I force myself to look back at my game and realize that while I've been lusting after Doc, QuikSilver has somehow outmaneuvered me on the board.

"Fuck," I mutter, searching for a way out. I knew this might happen, but it still sucks to lose.

"Having problems?" Doc asks.

She finally looks at me, a sweet but tart smile playing on her mouth. Like she's happy I'm in trouble.

"No," I say shortly. "At least nothing I can't handle."

I resign the game since I can't see any way to win, then flip on the AI. We're playing best out of five, and I mean to take the next four games without a sweat. And to stop sweating over Doc, although I'm way more likely to win than to do that.

QuikSilver starts off with a very predictable strategy, which makes my teeth grind. They're better than this, and my AI won't learn anything from this kind of play. It's like they know what I'm doing and are trying to piss me off.

"Play better," I say through my teeth.

"What?"

"Nothing."

"Oh? Because it sounded like you were having problems. Again."

Okay, there's no mistake now—she's baiting me. And looking pretty pleased about it. Which of course makes my cock respond.

Fuck. I am an idiot about this woman.

I shift in my seat, focusing back on my game. "I'm not."

I am though, and if this keeps up, all my test runs tonight will be worthless.

"Really?"

There's a challenge in her voice, one that sparks along my skin. I want to get up from this desk and show her exactly what I want to do with that smart mouth and how I've got no problem kissing her until she begs for it.

She blinks once, long and slow, and I realize I've been staring at her like a dork.

"You seem awfully interested in my *problems*."

That catches her off guard. Her gaze flicks back to her display but doesn't focus on it. "No. I've got my own work, and you won't stop talking."

I see the headphones sitting next to her left hand and

smile. She could have put them on at any moment and ignored me.

But she didn't. And maybe, just maybe, she's been noticing me as much as I've been noticing her.

The game clock on my screen goes red and flashing. "Fuck." My hands jump back to the keyboard, and I set down my game piece before the time for my turn expires. If I'd missed the turn, I would have forfeited the game.

I don't like to lose. Makes me surly.

We go a few more moves, QuikSilver keeping to their bullshit safe strategy. Then, about halfway through the game, their style changes, shifting into that chaotic brilliance I know and love.

My mouth twists with triumph, savage and bright. Yes, this is what I was searching for. The AI stumbles over the next few moves, confused by the change. I let it make the mistakes because that's the only way it'll ever learn.

QuikSilver slows down, takes their time making their own moves. They must have sensed the change in play and are trying to adjust.

Two more moves and my AI catches on, making a move that sets up a winning strategy. As long as QuikSilver doesn't see our intentions and block us.

I release a low, satisfied breath. I run my tongue along my teeth, already tasting my victory. If I take the next four games, I'll pull out the bottle of añejo tequila sitting in the bottom drawer of this desk and pour myself a glass. Maybe even convince the good doctor to join me.

I glance over at her and immediately regret it. She's got the tip of her tongue tucked into the corner of her mouth, her gaze tight and focused, and my dick goes hard.

Maybe I'll take my tequila home and jerk off by myself. Because while I might, *might* convince her to share a drink with me, she'd laugh in my face if I suggested she come home with me.

But if I can convince her… *How* I'd convince her…

The game timer flashes red at me again. Whoops. Let myself get distracted by her. Again.

I make the move the AI suggests, then wait. Soon enough I'm caught back up in the rhythms of the game, pulling off the AI's strategy flawlessly. QuikSilver doesn't have a clue, and in a few moves, it will all be over.

And then, at move fifty, it all comes crashing down.

"Fuck." I say it so softly I can barely hear myself. I can barely believe what I'm seeing.

I thought QuikSilver was playing defensively—erratically but defensively—and they never saw the web my AI was spinning for them. But when they set down their piece at move fifty, I see that they've had their own web, and my AI and I were both too blind to see it.

"Son of a bitch." I whisper it, but by the time I reach the end, it's bursting out of me. "Son. Of. A. Bitch."

A tiny laugh catches my attention. It's over almost as soon as it starts, but make no mistake—Doc was laughing. Right as I lost that last game.

Suddenly it all hits me. I might be a genius, but like I said, when it comes to her, I'm a fucking idiot. And I should have figured this out long ago.

She's QuikSilver. My nemesis.

CHAPTER 2

"Had fun beating me, huh?"

At Finn's question, I go stiff. *Oh shit.*

Okay, so yeah, I've been stalking him in the Go forums for a while, playing him every chance I get. He's a great opponent: prone to shortsightedness but able to pull off brilliant moves to get out of sticky situations.

I never let him know that it was me playing him though. He already has a massive ego to go with his massive muscles. And I don't need to be thinking about *that*, not with him so close I can touch him, close enough that all I can smell is his soap. It's piney with a hint of something deeper, darker…

And there I go again. I take a deep breath and try to lean away, out of his shadow.

I always forget how big he is. Although he's reminding me really hard right now, looming over me. After I was dumb enough to laugh, he marched over to my workstation, all aggrieved male ego.

Poor baby.

My heart dances into my throat, which is super inconvenient since I need to say something. Only nothing coherent is coming to me.

"I don't know what you're talking about." I can't make

that even a little bit confident, so it falls flatter than a pancake.

Finn clearly thinks it's weak too. He's not even looking at my computer screen, but I can tell from his expression he knows everything. Including about the AI I've been using to play against him.

"I expected better from you." He sighs, which makes his chest get even bigger. "You know exactly what I'm talking about, and it doesn't suit you to lie about it."

That's the trouble with Finn—he's arrogant and infuriating, but he's never treated me like I'm dumb. Which is rare in the tech world, especially for a man as smart as he is.

"Okay." I lift my hands. "I admit it—I'm the one who's been playing you all this time." I can't help my grin, because not only have I been playing him, I've been beating him. Often. "Would you like some pointers on your play? Your ability to think long-term is shit. But you already know that."

He doesn't grin back, which is rare for him. He's either angrier with me than he's letting on… or he's being serious for once.

I'd rather he be angry—I'd have to take Serious Finn… well, seriously. I like having him at arm's length. Finn in close quarters would be dangerous to my health.

"And sometimes your moves are too erratic to match your personality," he says. "Tell me, how long have you been working on that AI that you set on me?"

"How long have you been working on your AI?" I counter.

He crosses his massive arms, emphasizing how wide his chest is. He's wearing a button-down shirt, open at the collar and the sleeves rolled up to his elbows. The poor, strained fabric can barely contain the mass of him—all that muscle and hair and the sheer, aggressive masculinity that crackles off him.

I suppose that's another reason I always find myself

poking at him. In an industry notorious for bad male behavior, he insists on being the most masculine guy in the room. He's got a long, thick beard, close-cropped hair that's almost a buzz cut, and muscles that can only come from an intense weight lifting regime.

I'm not attracted to guys like him. I'm not. He's just too close to me right now—that's why my body is popping and humming.

He narrows his eyes. "How do you know about my AI?"

I hold my triumph inside. I wasn't exactly certain he had an AI, but now he's confirmed it—an unforced error on his part.

"It plays differently than you," I say. "It thinks further ahead, and it isn't as brilliant"—I clear my throat hard—"it isn't as arrogant as you are."

He sets one hip against my desk, arms still crossed, everything about him emphasizing the power differential between us. The dark fabric of his pants pulls tight against the muscles of his thighs, which are thickly tensed. "I'm brilliant, huh?"

Oh God. I roll my eyes—there's that undented arrogance again. My brother was the same way about his intelligence, thinking he could conquer the world solely through his brain. Until the illness lurking beneath broke out and took over.

I force out a short breath. Finn might remind me of Ray, really painfully remind me of him, but I can't let my guard down here. "You know that you are. You don't need me to tell you that."

"No, I don't." He grins. "But it's always nice to hear."

I snort. Not very elegantly but he's not elegant himself, so I don't worry about it.

"Why are you working on an AI?" he asks.

"I could ask you the same." In fact, I'm desperate to ask him about it. He's a venture capitalist, not a programmer. At least not anymore. Before, he was more famous as a hacker than a programmer, breaking into systems and messing with them just to prove he could. There's a rumor he used to break into the NSA system on the regular and leave annoying memes on all their computers. I can definitely believe it.

Ray used to do unsolved math theorems for fun. Not as exciting as hacking the NSA, but Ray wasn't a rule breaker.

Isn't. I correct myself furiously, silently.

Finn shrugs. "I get bored."

Of course. Someone like him would *get bored* and decide to use this amazing lab with all these toys to develop a machine that can think. All for shits and giggles.

Finn is here, playing in his own private kingdom, and Ray, who's just as brilliant, is in prison. Simply because Ray came up with the losing ticket in the genetic lottery.

It makes all the work I put into my own AI seem silly. Heck, it makes my entire life and my family seem silly, point-less. I tamp down my jealousy since I know my AI is good—it beat his a few minutes ago. And it's not Finn's fault Ray got sick.

"I guess being super-duper rich just doesn't keep you busy enough."

His expression is pleased, like I've figured something out. "I need a lot of stimulation."

I want to laugh, because it's such a ridiculous double entendre, like a fifteen-year-old's idea of seduction. And he knows it's ridiculous. But he already gets enough ego strokes in life, so I don't.

He shifts on the edge of the desk, the muscles in his thighs playing like tiger cubs—Jesus, what is wrong with me that I'm thinking that? "So, why are you designing an AI?" he asks. "It doesn't seem like something January would need."

It's true. The company I work for, Ultra Encryption, does

security stuff, protecting people's information and data. No AI needed.

I'm not working on this program because I'm bored… but I did want something to work on that was all my own, that wouldn't need to be delivered on a certain date or coded to a customer's specifications. I wanted something that was only what *I* wanted.

What with everything going on with Ray's legal appeals, I needed something that had a chance of actually succeeding. Even if it was only making a computer win a game or two against a human.

"This isn't for Ultra," I say. "I'm working on it on my own."

"Oh yeah?" He tries to lean over to see the monitor. I tilt it away from him. "You got a specific market in mind? Maybe launching your own start-up?"

"I'm thinking about… Well, a lot of stuff. It has a lot of applications."

It's a weaselly, corporate-speak answer, but I'm almost ashamed of the real reason because it's so goody-goody.

He's probably working on his AI to better sell shit to people. Yeah, he's bored, but he also makes money like he breathes. He can't not do it.

And I'm working on my AI for something noble and progressive. The tech world claims to like those things in theory but, in practice, not so much.

To distract him from my nonanswer, I say, "I can't believe you're taking time out of your busy schedule of making tons of money to invent an AI just for fun."

He raises his eyebrows, which makes him even more devastatingly handsome. "Oh no. I'll pass this off to some start-up in our stable once it's ready, let them develop it for more business-facing stuff. Predicting consumer behavior, stuff like that."

My heart sinks. Even something he began as a thought

experiment, something to keep his too-big brain busy, is going to be used to make money. I shouldn't be so disappointed. He is, after all, a billionaire. People like him don't get to where they are by being altruistic.

Which is too bad, because Ray could use some altruism, specifically in the form of some money for his legal fees. I've tapped out my own account and taken loans from friends, and I still can't keep up with the bills. But I can't leave Ray in prison—for schizophrenics, prison is the worst place to be. Not that it's a picnic for anyone else.

"So." Finn closes the distance between us, putting us *Wow, this is really intimate* inches apart. My focus snaps tight on him. "When can I see your source code?"

I close my mouth. It wouldn't be that big of a deal to show him, but… it would feel that way to me. He's hot, he's a genius, and he's also incredibly arrogant. Tangling with him would be like defusing a bomb—yeah, it'd get your heart working and the adrenaline surging, but if you screw up, it's kaboom.

"Hmm." A smile teases at the corners of his mouth. "I gotta work for it?"

My entire body flushes. He makes it sound like he's going to seduce it out of me, which my body wouldn't be averse to. But my body is stupid when it comes to him. My mind knows all the reasons why not, but my body doesn't know any of that. My body only knows that his body would feel amazing next to mine, his strong, clever fingers against my clit would be devastating, and that beard abrading my skin as his tongue tasted me would be heavenly.

"It's not a question of work," I say. "It's just none of your business."

"I'll show you mine if you show me yours."

That catches me but good. To see his source code… it'd be like getting a peek at da Vinci's sketchbook.

"I don't think so," I say, but I can hear the fluster in my voice.

So can he. "You like games, don't you? Of course you do—you've been playing games with me for months now, haven't you?"

I don't bother to answer that.

"How about we play for it?"

I'm not going to be lured in like this. I just won't let myself. "Right," I say slowly. "If I win, I don't have to tell you anything. Those are the rules, right? Yeah, I'd rather not. With those rules, I can also win by just not playing."

"I was thinking more along the lines of truth or dare." His eyes darken. "You know that game."

I can't help but let my gaze wander slowly over him. I was right when I figured he'd try to seduce it out of me. Truth or dare between two people with an atmosphere as charged as ours isn't a game—it's foreplay.

"I don't know how to play truth or dare," I say primly. Which is kind of true; I've never actually played it. But I have a pretty good idea what it entails.

"The rules are easy, almost as easy as Go. I ask a question, and you either have to tell me the truth or take a dare. And then you get to do the same to me."

The way he says that makes me think of all the things I can do to him in return, the way I can make his body go crazy—revenge for the way he makes me feel.

When I find his gaze, he knows he's got me snared. I love beating this man even if he doesn't know it's me who's beating him. This time I can infuriate him to his face and keep my secrets to myself.

"The dares can't involve me taking off my clothes," I say quickly.

"I'm a gentleman; I wouldn't dream of it."

He's not a gentleman at all—he's a Bastard. And proud of

it. But I have faith he'll keep his word. His ego's too big to allow him to not keep his promises.

I nod. "All right then. You got a question—what am I doing with my AI? And I choose a dare."

He shakes his head. "No, that wasn't my question. That was before the game started, and it doesn't count. My real question is this: Why are you testing your AI here?"

That's an easy one. He already knows the answer. "Because I want to use the servers. We don't have computing power like this in our offices. Which you knew."

"Just getting a baseline," he says idly.

He thinks he's so damn clever, like he's going to use this game to pry information out of me. I see red for a moment, then force myself to breathe it out.

"Okay, here's my question—why are you harassing me?"

His eyes widen at my open attack. I admit it's a little much, but he's so close I've been able to smell nothing but his soap and skin, and it's starting to drive me a little crazy. Actually, a lot crazy.

"You're the one who was stalking me across the Go forums." His voice drops a degree, but he doesn't move away. "Never letting on who you really were."

Guilt makes my cheeks go cold.

"That wasn't an answer," I say to hide my reaction.

"No, it wasn't. I choose a dare."

A dare? When we started this game, I hadn't even considered I'd have to give *him* a dare. Suddenly the only things I can think of are dirty, perverse, exactly the kind of things I was afraid he might suggest to me.

He smiles slow and wicked at my confusion. "You know, you can dare me to take my clothes off." He raises his hand to the first button on his shirt. The chest hair thrusting out hooks on his index finger, and I can only imagine what it would feel like under my fingers as I run my hands along his chest. "The only rule was that I couldn't make *you* take your clothes off."

"I don't..." I lick my suddenly dry lips. I know I'm giving too much away, but my brain is working harder than an overloaded circuit. "I don't want to see you naked." I say that so faintly he can probably smell the lie before I've finished.

"Really? You don't think about me naked?"

I shake my head wildly.

He leans closer, his hand still playing with his shirt button. "Even just kissing me—have you wondered about that?"

I can't look away from his fingers. "I don't wonder about kissing strange men."

"Good. I'm glad I'm not a stranger then."

I close my eyes for half a heartbeat. "This is inappropriate."

He ignores me. "I mean, I imagine kissing *you*. All the time."

I blink up at him. "You do?"

I'm not some innocent—I've had my fair share of serious relationships—but I've never had a man admit so baldly that he fantasizes about me. It makes my knees do funny things. Thank God I'm already sitting down.

"Of course. I imagine how it would feel sliding my hand through your hair, cupping the back of your head, tilting your face up toward mine, your neck all long and pretty as I do."

Oh God. I can see it too clearly, my entire body tightening in response yet also going liquid at the same time. Tight liquid, which makes no sense, which proves how badly he can scramble my brain.

He's not done though. "And then once I have your mouth right where I want it, I'll learn every millimeter of it."

Millimeter. God, so much smaller than inches, so much more detailed, so much sexier.

"You never think about that?" His voice is so dark and sweet I swear I taste chocolate. "Me kissing you, and how I'll take my time with it, bring my *flashes of brilliance* to it?"

Of course I have, which is exactly the problem. Dammit, I never should've chased him across all those Go forms, never should have tested my AI against his. I should have run the first moment I saw him.

Suddenly I realize that I'm sprawled in my chair, my legs wide open as if inviting him in. I was so lost in the fantasy he was spinning I completely lost control of myself.

In a flash, I smack off the workstation, not giving a shit about shutting it down properly. In the next breath I'm snapping up, sending my chair sailing out behind me. And then I'm grabbing every bit of my work that I can and shoving it haphazardly into my bag.

"I'm working on an AI to do remote diagnostics for people in areas that don't have a doctor. Sort of an AI medical assistant." I say that so fast I trip over my own tongue.

And then I'm escaping out the door, never looking back at him. It's only when I'm inside my car, my shaking hands trying to turn the key in the ignition, that I realize I forfeited.

He won.

CHAPTER 3

I get to see Doc again on Tuesday, which makes me happier than it should.

She's at Bastard Capital with the Ultra Encryption team, giving all the partners—meaning us, the Bastards—an update on Ultra's latest system.

January is at the front of the conference room, going on about encryption and chips. It's usually stuff that I eat up, but somehow I can't do anything but think about Doc.

She won't look at me. It's deliberate, because as much as her gaze wanders around the room, it never once lands on me. She's ignoring me as hard as I'm concentrating on her. Like my head is just buzzing with her—the way her skirt rustles as she shifts in her chair, the skirt that's cradling her thighs right now. The scuffle of her shoes on the floor, low heeled with pointy toes in a color of pink so hot it should be illegal. They're shoes that say *hell yes, look at my feet* in a way that's very different from a stiletto but just as compelling. The motions of her hands as she makes notes, her fingers long, graceful, but also determined. She takes notes the old-fashioned way with a pen and paper while everyone else is typing away.

Smart to do it that way. Your brain retains things better

when you write them down.

Not that her brain needs any help. I tell myself I'm only going to talk to her about what's in her brain, not about her body and how mine reacts to it. I've almost convinced myself I'm telling the truth.

While I've been daydreaming about Doc, the meeting has been going on without me. The great thing about having an update meeting with your partner's girlfriend is that you can fuck around with your friends while pretending to do business.

Not that I mind more serious meetings, but I'd rather cut loose if given the chance. And since January, Mark's fiancée, is giving us the update along with her team, I don't have to keep my mouth shut and pretend to be the serious one. The Bastards already have a *serious one.*

The Bastards are me, hacker extraordinaire and all-around genius; Mark, our deals guy; Logan, the details lover; Paul, the old-money guy; Elliot, our lawyer; and Dev, the mysterious visionary. Of course we play up some of those aspects for the media since it definitely helps our PR. But there's more than a kernel of truth in these roles we've taken.

"So where are we with the Pixio deliveries?" Mark asks. "And when can we pitch them the new chip?"

January shakes her head. "The testing hasn't been going well. I don't know when we'll have a timeline for pitching that."

"Okay, I'll plan for chip pitches by month's end."

January gives him an exasperated look. "That's not what I said at all."

He smiles sweetly at her. "But I know you'll have it ready in a month."

The compliment has January flushing and looking down like she's a shy schoolgirl.

Next to me, Paul rolls his eyes. I'm half tempted to do it myself. "Could you two get a room?" he says.

I could add my two cents, but I decide to keep it professional. Doc already doesn't think much of me, but I'll show her I can behave myself in a meeting. Sometimes.

Across the table, Logan laughs softly, his eyes on his phone.

"Are you texting your wife?" Elliot asks. He and Logan are brothers, so Elliot's the only one who can get away with that question. Logan's wife, Callie, is pregnant, and they've only just recently reconciled after a bitter separation, so we're trying to go easy on them. Not scare her off with our loving insults.

Logan never would have answered texts in a meeting before Callie came back. Now he's leaving work early and taking the weekends off. It's crazy.

I wonder what that's like: to love someone so much you're willing to give up a thing that has defined and driven you for so long. Logan used to be a fucking machine when it came to business, and now he's… softer. Happier. I mean, he's still a Bastard, just less of a *bastard*.

Doc rustles her papers, catching my attention. Someone who spends her free time designing AIs doesn't do it for the money. She does it for the love of building things, of getting inside something and figuring out how it works. I can respect the hell out of that, and I do.

I respect her, and I want to fuck her. Hell of a combination.

When the meeting adjourns and she heads for the door, I put on some speed to catch her before she leaves. It's just a little too much speed, enough to startle her, but she has no reason to be afraid. I'm only going to talk about her brain. Her big, beautiful brain.

I catch her just before she reaches the door, putting my hand against the wall to block her in with my arm. She pulls in a sharp breath, more surprised than scared.

"Let's talk," I say. I keep it low so that only she can hear.

She licks her lips, and her eyelids flutter like I've just run my tongue over her neck.

I wait until everyone's left the room, leaving my hand in place to keep her right next to me. I'm well aware of the effect my size has on people, particularly women, so I don't usually use it as an intimidation tactic. But I know Doc can hold her own with me. With a well-placed insult and a sharp glance, she can prick me hard enough to hurt. That she's not doing so now is telling.

Instead, she's watching me, her whiskey-brown eyes intense behind her glasses. I can see why she wouldn't look at me during the meeting. This is a woman who's got more than encryption keys on her mind.

Once we're alone, she looks pointedly at my arm and then at the door.

I flex my hand against the wall.

"Is that supposed to draw attention to your biceps?" she asks.

"Have you been looking at my biceps?"

"When you're constantly flexing them in people's faces, it's hard not to notice."

I snort. "You're the only person who's commented on my biceps."

She pouts, plumping out her lower lip. I want to test that softness with my teeth, then delve my tongue into her mouth when she moans with pleasure.

Brain. I'm supposed to only be thinking about her brain.

"Maybe people aren't commenting because they're embarrassed for you." Her gaze runs over me. "Clearly you want people to notice, but maybe they can't find much to comment on."

I dip my head toward hers. "Seems to me last night you were the only one who was embarrassed. All flushed and flustered when we were only playing a game."

"You suggested taking your clothes off," she hisses.

"You brought it up first."

"Because I knew that's where your mind would go."

"And yet it's where your mind went too," I say, smooth as the silk of her skirt. "But what I really want to talk about is your AI."

She tilts her head back so she can look me square in the eye. "It's not for sale. And no, I don't care how much you offer. Not everything in this world has a price tag."

"I never said anything about buying it. All I want is to talk about it."

Okay, maybe I did have some idea about buying it, about using it for a start-up. Maybe even setting her up with her own company.

But I'm also curious—I want to climb inside her lines of code and see how they work. It's probably my worst fault, my curiosity. And also my best trait. It's gotten me into trouble more times than I can count over the years and also made me more money than I can count. So I like to indulge it whenever I can.

Intellectual curiosity, of course. My physical curiosity about how she'll taste, how she'll feel as she moves beneath me, will have to remain unsatisfied. She's made that more than clear even if she's staring at me as hard as I'm staring at her.

"You want to just look at my code then?" She raises a skeptical eyebrow, that simple question suddenly become something filthy.

Oh yes, I'd like to look at your code. All stripped down and naked, bared to me.

I clear my throat. "Look, we're both working on an AI to play Go. Aren't you the least bit curious to compare what we've each done?"

Her gaze cuts away, and she blinks once, twice. Oh yeah, she definitely is.

Then her expression hardens. "I'm only doing an experiment, something fun. Just like you. I don't need you to come look at it."

As if I was going to grade her on it or something. "What was that about a remote doctor though?"

She bites her lip, and her shoulders sag as she turns to face me fully. "Can you just forget I said that?"

"No, I can't. People have been interested in medical videoconferencing and stuff like that for a while, but it's never really taken off."

"Hmm, I wonder why."

There's so much sarcasm in that I can taste it, all tart on my tongue. "You mean the profit motive behind health care," I ask, "which makes it almost impossible for rural medical providers to make an actual living?"

She looks like I've started spouting Greek. "Um, yes. Exactly that, actually."

"We had to drive an hour to get to an ER when I was a kid," I say. "Doctor visits weren't a thing."

Thank God we were all mostly healthy and the county clinic—only an hour and a half away—provided vaccinations. If you had an ear infection, persistent cough, anything that wasn't gonna kill you immediately, you just sucked it up.

"I'll bet a kid like you had to make the drive to the ER pretty often." There's a hint of a smile on her face.

"I tried to keep my injuries to minor ones, but yeah."

Nobody in my hometown has to drive that far anymore. We've got a brand-new hospital, doctors up the wazoo, and a free clinic for anybody who needs it. All funded by a very generous anonymous donor. Because only assholes would donate in order to plaster their name across the side of a fucking hospital.

Something shifts in Doc's face. Her expression opens, just a crack. "I was thinking about a medical AI," she says. "Something way better than using Dr. Google to diagnose yourself with bubonic plague or something."

I nod but keep my mouth shut. I want her to keep going.

"It would be great for people without access to a doctor or even people who simply can't afford to go. A friend of mine in med school once said he'd be a very highly trained algorithm by the time he finished, and that stuck with me."

"It sounds very noble."

She tilts a skeptical face toward me. "You make noble sound like a bad thing."

"Look, just because I'm good at making money, doesn't mean I don't want to give back." Everybody in this town has their pet charity except for maybe Arne Fuchs. We've had several run-ins with that asshole before, and trust me, he'd start a foundation for the kicking of puppies, sole beneficiary himself.

"I thought you were the trickster of the group." Her skepticism is even sharper now.

It's all true. I do tend to think about things in terms of what they'll bring me either via my bottom line or my own amusement. But suddenly I'm tempted to tell her about my hometown, about how it started dirt-poor and went downhill from there and about my attempts to make it livable again.

I hold back though. There's a reason my name isn't on any of the buildings or places that I paid for in my hometown. Hell, I can rename the entire town after myself if I want, given how much I've donated.

But like I said, I didn't do it for the ego strokes.

I clear my throat. "I'm serious. If you're interested in starting something with AI medical diagnostics, I can get you set up. The team, funding—"

She holds up a hand. "I never said I wanted any of that. I'm happy working for January. And working on my AI on my own time, on my own terms."

"Of course it would be on your own terms. I'm not gonna force you to do anything." I relax my shoulders, trying to look smaller than I am. "Really, all I want is to get a look at the program. You've really got something there."

"I bet you do," she says coolly. "It'd be nice to get a look at the nuts and bolts of the AI that beat yours, wouldn't it? Maybe you can even take some of those nuts and bolts and put it on your own machine. Make it more valuable."

I take a step back. "Right, because what you do at Ultra is all charity work. And not a way to monetize security."

Her smile is slow and sweet and dark, like hot molasses. "It burns you up that I won't show you, doesn't it? You're the genius, the one who gets his ego fondled every chance he can, and it just riles you up I'm not doing it, isn't it? Your ego is so big everybody has to get a stroke in, don't they?"

I mirror her smile, letting my arms settle deeper against my chest. "Well, my ego is pretty big, but I'm particular about who gets to stroke it."

Her cheeks turn the most gorgeous shade of rose, and I savor the moment when I've finally, finally won a point against her.

"Are we finished?" The tartness is gone, replaced by a gorgeous flutter. "I really don't have time for this—I've got somewhere I need to be."

I check the display on the wall. Dammit, she's right; I've got somewhere I need to be too. Our playtime will have to wait. I lift my arm and gesture gallantly to the door. "I didn't mean to keep you waiting."

"But you did," she snaps. The blush hasn't left her cheeks, and she's breathing a little too hard.

"Think about letting me get *intimate* with your program," I call after her as she marches out.

I can't quite hear what she mutters under her breath, but it sounds something like *when hell freezes over.*

I smile, because if anyone can devise a way to freeze hell over, it's me.

CHAPTER 4

The weather is awful, it's a Friday night, and this protest was completely unscheduled, which means that a turnout of several hundred people is pretty awesome.

I'm in the middle of the crowd that the cops have penned in an empty lot across from the Oakland police headquarters, where the department has set up a podium, chairs, VIPs, and a few news cameras. It's a shiny, focused kind of bustle that has people on the street stopping and staring for a few moments, then going on about their business. It is, like I said, Friday night—work's done and everyone's got better things to do.

That's why the police department called this press conference for right now, because their new crime prevention panopticon is pretty unpopular and they're hoping to slip the announcement of its launch past the public without any fuss.

But we still came to make a fuss. I'm not the type you normally see at a protest, even with my purple hair, but I'm here to make noise about Ray, hopefully get some publicity for his case. I've got my sign held high above my head, with his picture and name, and demand that his case be retried. The cops filling the streets and the plaza across from us probably won't take a first look at my sign, much less a second one, but I have to try.

Several people hold up signs declaring Corvus to be Big Brother—Corvus is the company providing the equipment and software for the shiny new panopticon, and they also tried to take down Ultra Encryption a while back—but I'm the only one holding one up for Ray.

Ray is my twin. He's always been smart, probably too smart for his own good, but unlike me, he didn't take stuff apart to see how it worked. He preferred to explore things in his mind, spending hours just sitting and thinking. We knew from the beginning he'd be a genius.

Sure enough, when I went off to UC Santa Cruz, Ray went off to MIT. He sailed through his bachelor's degree—pure math—and when he came back home to do his graduate work at Berkeley, I was so happy for him. He was close to me again, and he was going to have an amazing academic career.

Then everything started to go wrong. The voices started, then the hallucinations. He took the medications the psychiatrists gave him, hoping it would help him finish his PhD. At first.

But the side effects of the meds—he gained so much weight I could hardly recognize him, and the tremors were so bad he couldn't use a computer—were almost as bad as the disease itself. And his thinking got so fuzzy he couldn't work on his thesis.

So Ray stopped his meds. You always tell yourself that you'd never let your brother hit rock bottom, that you'd never let him sleep on the streets, but when people say that, they have no idea how powerless they really are. I couldn't force Ray to stay in school. I couldn't help him keep a job. And in the end, I couldn't force him to live with me.

I thought that my brother being homeless was the worst that could happen, but I was wrong. Ray being convicted of armed robbery was much, much worse. Ray had become a fixture in his neighborhood in Oakland, with the residents keeping an eye out for him as best they could. I visited him each day too. There was a drugstore that he bought snacks and cigarettes from nearly every day. One day the drugstore was robbed at gunpoint. Ray said he didn't do it, the store clerk said the robber wasn't Ray, but the police had Ray on a city-owned security camera going into the drugstore around the time of the robbery. And so they pinned the crime on my brother and sent him to prison for almost a decade.

Holding a sign at this protest is one of the smallest things I've done to get my brother released, but it's still something. I doubt we'll get justice for Ray or stop the panopticon, but at least we're trying.

The chief of police is up at the podium, small and blue and blurry from this distance. But they've amplified her voice so we can hear her speech. She goes on about how amazing it will be to have cameras everywhere, watching everyone in the city, and using Corvus's amazing technology to predict and prevent crimes before they even happen.

"Booo." The noise comes from every belly in the crowd, a deep vibration of anger and objection. The chief keeps going on about how wonderful the program is, completely ignoring us.

So that's where we're at now. The police department is talking about throwing people in jail for crimes they think they might commit before they even happen. Which is even worse than what they did to Ray. It's chilling and horrible and something right out of a dystopian movie, and the chief is so damn chirpy about it that it makes my teeth hurt.

But there's a large mass of people behind these barricades, all of them shouting that no, we won't let this happen. Not without a fight. We have rights, and we'll keep demanding them.

I chant louder, wanting to drown out the chief's drivel. I know I can't, but I try anyway.

They haven't given the protesters a ton of space, so we're packed in shoulder to knee like sardines, only louder and more pissed off. On the other side of the barricade, there's a line of police all decked out in riot gear, reminding us that even without the cameras or the computer programs, they still hold all the power here. If they decide we're too far out of line, it'll be cracked skulls and broken noses. I've seen that happen before, although thankfully it's never been my skull or nose.

I shift and accidentally step on someone's toes. "Sorry," I say to the girl behind me. She's wearing a medic's armband and a big backpack, which probably has all her emergency supplies.

"No worries." She flashes me a quick grin. "Hopefully that's the only injury I see tonight."

The chief finishes up her speech to some very polite applause, then steps down from the podium. She doesn't take any questions even though the press is lobbing them at her like hand grenades. The chief is smiling as she goes back to her seat and greets the person waiting there—

I do a double take when I see who it is. Even from this distance, I recognize that fuck-you-I'm-untouchable posture —Minerva Dyne, Arne Fuchs's favorite hatchet woman.

I knew Corvus was behind this, but I'm still surprised to see her there, shaking the mayor's hand and offering congratulations. I've had run-ins with Minerva before, back when Fuchs was trying to put Ultra out of business.

The both of them are shady characters, avoiding anywhere there might be publicity. All these news cameras can't be good for Minerva's complexion—she thrives in the shadows. The fact that she's so intimately involved with this program that she actually came to the event makes the panopticon that much more sinister.

But there's not much I can do about it except exercise my right to protest. So I chant even louder, stomping my feet and shaking my fist at the press conference. The police can't yet predict what crimes I might commit, and I have a right to protest. So I'm going to take full advantage.

"Yeah," the dude next to me shouts, stomping his feet. "Scream your lungs out at those assholes." He's in a polo and khakis and looks like he just finished his middle-management shift in retail. I smile and give him a thumbs-up, which he returns.

Someone I don't know takes to the podium and thanks everyone for coming. With that, the chief and all the dignitaries rise and leave, never glancing over at us even once. I shake my sign at them anyway.

The press is a little better, with some of the news cameras actually panning over us. But I'm wondering if the press will even mention that we were here, that someone was speaking out against this. Usually they don't, not unless a protest gets really rowdy.

Once the last of the press leaves, there's a shift in the line of police facing us, like a current has gone through them, snapping them awake. The hair on the back of my neck rises.

The entire line of them takes one step back in unison, then another, sounding more like storm troopers on the march than peacekeepers. They don't do anything else, but my sense of unease rises anyway, tight at the back of my neck and pooling deep in my belly. It doesn't feel like they're backing away to give us space.

"Shit," I mutter under my breath. I glance over at khaki guy, who looks as uneasy as I am. The medic has disappeared, which sucks, because if those cops charge us…

But the cops don't do anything else. The protesters deflate some, the air of righteous anger passing out of us since it's over and we all need to file out of here. Once the cops open up the barricades, we can do that. I'm a little surprised at all the barricades and riot gear for such a small protest, but maybe they're not taking any chances with how badly they want this panopticon program to stay quiet.

One of the barricades comes down, and the entire crowd shifts, everyone trying to angle themselves toward that opening. There's no point sticking around, and our "free speech area" is starting to feel more like a cage.

As I shuffle toward the narrow exit—seriously, I get that they don't want us just spilling into the streets, but they could take a couple more barriers down—I glance over at the line of police. I can't see their expressions behind their face shields, but their posture remains on edge. Which is weird, because we're dispersing peacefully. Unless maybe they're mad we're ruining their Friday night—

Something flies through the air toward the line of police. A rock or something hard and dark that's close to the same size—and it came from behind the police line. Not from us protesters.

It hits one of their helmets with a deep, echoing thunk. The officer stumbles, almost going down.

Everything shifts then. I can taste the impending disaster in the air, sharp and coppery.

It wasn't us. But the cops won't believe that.

Suddenly their line melts and they're coming toward us. I can't tell what they mean to do—arrest some people, kettle us somewhere—but the crowd isn't waiting to find out. When the police move, the protest crowd dissolves into panicked chaos.

Everyone's bolting for the one exit, pressure building as more and more people surge forward, but the exit isn't getting any bigger. My heart can barely pump I'm being squeezed so hard, and my lungs are burning.

One of the barriers falls beneath the crowd's feet with a sharp clatter. People rush into the open area, and suddenly I have enough room to breathe again, gasping like a fish on a dock.

The police are moving too, protesters dodging them as they try to escape into one of the side streets. The space I had is quickly consumed again by a press of bodies as we fall back from the police.

I can't move because I'm being swept up in a wave of people. There are elbows in my sides, knees in my thighs, and shoulders trying to press me under. My heart is loud in my ears as I fight to grab a full breath, trying to get oxygen to my panicking brain. I have to get out of this crowd, find a backstreet, a quiet place to reassess and figure out how to get out of here. If I don't, if I fall, I could die.

My poster is torn out of my hand by someone's arm or leg. I can't see which—I only catch one last glimpse of it as I'm swept forward, a boot on the side of Ray's face. And then it's gone beneath a dozen more feet.

Someone is shouting something, but I can't tell if they're calling for help, telling people to stop, showing people where to go—I can't discern anything but the pressure of the crowd, pushing me wherever it wants to go.

I can't see the police, but I know they're still there. I see one of the fallen barriers ahead and an open space just beyond, somehow miraculously clear of people in the strange way of a thoughtless crowd. I aim for it, pushing myself forward with my elbows, trying to break free, but it's no use. The crowd carries me along as if I were driftwood, battering me every time I try to fight it.

Still I fight. An elbow here, a shoulder there, planting my feet to resist. I get an elbow in return, a hair pull, my scalp screaming until I'm loose.

It's not enough. The crowd shifts, and there are the police again, dragging off anyone they can catch. In a few seconds, one of them will grab me unless I can get loose of this crowd. But at my back is another barricade—I've gotten turned around—and surrounding me is the crowd.

The crowd, the police, or that bit of open space: those are my choices.

I set my shoulders and aim for the open patch. This time I manage to move against the crowd. I get a whack to my shin, a punch to my ribs that makes me wheeze, but I push forward. I ache all over, but my heart is pumping with triumph. I'm going to make it.

But I don't.

One last shove and I'll be there, safe and free of the crowd. My heels leave the ground… and they don't find it again.

One second my feet are underneath me, and in the next the ground is heading toward me—fast, way too fast—and there's suddenly nothing for me to grab to stop myself. Both my hands close on emptiness, my palms brushing the asphalt as the rest of me follows them. My pulse hammers through my fingers, as strong as my panic.

I've been afraid a lot of times my life. But I'm never so afraid as I am in this moment, knowing that if I land, it will probably be the last thing I ever do.

All I can think about is the sign I brought, trampled beneath this crowd, Ray's face torn and battered, the same way I'll be when I hit the ground.

Only I don't land. Something snags me—an arm, it must be an arm, but my brain can't process that in my panic—and pulls me back against a massive body, knocking the wind out of me. I pant and blink, my mind racing to catch up to where I am now.

Safe. That's where I am.

There's an all-too-familiar growl in my ear, a familiar scent rising above the smell of panic thick in the air.

"Are you okay?" The voice is rough against my ear, but I've never been so happy to hear Finn's voice. I want to start crying, but instead I simply nod.

Safe. It's the only word I can think of, but I don't need to tell him that. He already knows he'll keep me safe.

"Let's get the fuck out of here," he says.

I couldn't agree more.

He carries me through the crowd, pushing his way through as if they were simply commuters on a busy side-walk instead of a panicked mass of humanity. He holds me tightly but gently, and I feel myself relax inch by inch, my muscles unwinding, my heart coming back to its normal rhythm. I can hear screaming and crying—the cracked skulls and broken noses are definitely happening—but it all feels outside the bubble Finn has placed me in.

Before I know it, he's gotten us both onto an empty side street where a car is already waiting. He climbs into the back seat of the Tesla, never letting go of me as he does.

As soon as the door slams shut, he's barking to the driver, "Get us out of here. My place. Now."

I don't even think to offer up my address or to protest his high-handedness. I simply let him take us wherever he wants to.

I'm so pissed off I could tear someone to pieces with my bare hands. Preferably the asshole who threw something at a line of fully suited-up riot cops.

Even though we're both in the back seat of my car and Doc is safe, the adrenaline surging through me demands a target, a neck between my fingers, a jaw under my fist.

Do not fuck with this woman, my inner beast keeps growling at everyone involved in that clusterfuck.

Thank God I was there and saw Doc in the crowd. I've been keeping an eye on Corvus—all the Bastards have—so I went to see what they were up to with this panopticon business. They seem to have moved on from simply spying on people to predicting if they're criminals before they even commit a crime.

The police chief droned on, the dignitaries applauded, and the press recorded it, and I didn't learn anything useful. I'd have to take a peek inside the Corvus system to see anything good, it seems. Corvus security is locked up tighter than a nun's knees at Chippendale's, so I'm going to have to get inventive if I want in. And I do.

The protest across the street was definitely more interesting than the cops' canned speeches. I noticed Doc among them as everyone was leaving, that flash of purple hair in the middle of a sea of boring browns and blacks like a beacon. So that was the appointment she was ditching me for after the meeting. I had to smile.

I'm not smiling right now, not with her bleeding and in shock next to me in the back seat. Stupid fucking idiot—who throws something at riot cops? And the cops—why charge like that? The missile or rock or whatever didn't even come from the protesters.

When the cops charged them and the protesters broke in a panic, I didn't even stop to think. In a flash, I ran for the barricades, hoisting myself up and over them. The cops didn't even try to stop me.

I wasn't paying much attention to them though. I was searching for Doc, desperate to find her before she could be trampled in that mass of humanity.

When I'd finally managed to catch up with her, she was already going down, falling beneath the feet of hundreds of stampeding people.

People talk about their heart stopping, but mine actually did, tripping over the sick fear flooding me. It was only by some miracle that I managed to catch her and pull her to safety.

Even now, the anger and fear is still running hot through me since she still looks so scared.

"What the hell were you doing there?" I growl. I don't intend to, but goddammit, she could have died. Right there in front of me, and I would have had to watch, helpless.

I don't do helpless, not since I was a kid. Not ever, really.

Doc decides to be her usual smart-mouthed self with me. "I was protesting. Do you know what that is, or should I call up my dictionary app for you?"

I'm too worked up to be sarcastic back. "You could have died. That entire situation was fucked."

She blinks hard, her gaze going unfocused. "I know. Oh God, I still feel like I'm falling."

I put my hand under her chin and tilt her face up so I can check out her eyes. Her pupils constrict as the light hits them, then widen as I pull her face closer to mine.

"Hey," I say gently as I can. "Stay with me." I angle my voice toward the driver. "Where's the nearest ER? We've got to get there—"

"No." Doc wraps her hand around my wrist, her fingers cold. "I don't need the ER."

"I don't believe you." Her skin is way too pale, the pulse in her throat hammering erratically against my knuckles. "If you're worried about the bill, I'll pay for all of it."

"That's not what I'm worried about." She shakes her head, but not hard enough to pull my hand away. "I'm only a little woozy."

I'm half tempted to take her in to get her checked out anyway, but I decide not to. Already her color's looking better, and she's breathing at a normal pace, if a little deeper than usual. Which is making her chest do interesting things, which I'm trying really hard not to fucking notice since she almost got trampled to death and all.

Which reminds me of how pissed I still am. "You know that protesting isn't going to do a damn thing to stop this panopticon?"

She would have died for absolutely nothing if she'd fallen there, and just the thought makes me want to punch something.

The look she flashes at me spits some of her old fire. "So what else am I supposed to do? Just let them set up some Big Brother surveillance thing without a peep?"

"There are other ways to fight."

"Like what? I'd love to hear how you're doing anything at all."

Okay, her color is definitely much better. Her cheeks are

flushed rose and her eyes are bright, and the animation in her expression is… way too attractive.

I look away, because the stuff that I am doing is all behind the scenes, very hush-hush, things I'm not telling anyone about. Hacking is best done in the dark with your mouth tightly shut. Hackers that brag about their shit often find themselves in jail.

So I change the subject. "You're spending the night at my place."

"What? No, I can go to my own house—"

I point to her hands, cutting her off. "Did you even notice that you're bleeding? The fact that you didn't means you need medical attention. Or just someone to take care of you."

She holds up her hands like she's seeing them for the first time ever. Her fingers are scraped, her palms are bloody, and there's a massive splinter in her thumb.

My rage surges up again. The Oakland chief of police is going to get a fucking earful from me about this. And I'm rich enough that she *has* to listen.

"You're going to my place," I say with firm finality. "Don't bother to argue. I'll bandage up your hands, and when I'm done, you can go home. If you feel well enough, okay?"

She's still staring at her hands. "I guess I can't bandage these myself," she says resignedly.

"Did you get hurt anywhere else?"

She gives me a sideways look as if I'm up to something, which I'm not. But then she twists her hands, catching sight of her palms, and she suddenly goes green. Her eyes flutter closed, and I only just catch her before she slumps onto the floor.

"Goddammit," I mutter to myself. "Steve," I call to the driver, "have a doctor meet us at my place."

She might not want to head to an ER, but I'll make damn sure she gets some kind of medical attention.

Doc shifts in my arms. "No," she says faintly. "Don't do

that. I just… I get a little woozy when it comes to blood. Especially my own blood."

"I'm used to it. My own blood," I explain at her puzzled look.

She studies my face, no doubt homing in on the scar under my right eye or the one slashing across my left cheek or the big one cutting right through my right eyebrow. I like driving off-road vehicles way too fast, and my body has the injuries to prove it.

"I bet you are," she murmurs, looking back at her hands. She's got gravel dug into one of her palms, which is going to be a bitch to clean. I'm going to have to hurt her when I dig that out, which makes my stomach twist.

"Fine, no doctor. But I'm going to nail that police chief's head to my office wall," I say, low and savage.

Her head flicks up in surprise. "You can do that?" Her expression drops. "Of course you can. You probably buy and sell city officials like it's nothing."

God, I only wish. "Not quite. But I've got an open line to the chief—shouldn't I use it?"

Her mouth tightens like she's struggling with something. "What were you even doing there?"

"I wanted to see what Corvus was up to." Keeping tabs on Corvus is something of mutual interest to us.

She sits up straight. "Minerva Dyne was there. Did you see her?"

"Oh yeah." Minerva is Arne Fuchs's assistant, although enforcer would probably be a better description. I definitely took notice of her.

"It means it's a high priority for him," Doc says excitedly. "He wouldn't send her if it wasn't. And if Fuchs is interested in this panopticon, it must be bad."

"I kind of figured that just from the description," I say dryly.

A smile flits across her face. "Yeah, even you should've

picked up on that." She moves her fingers and grimaces, going pale again.

I take both her hands in mine, careful to only touch her wrists where she's not injured. I rub slow circles there, being gentle with the delicate bones and tendons. Her skin is warm, and I can smell her shampoo, something flowery but not sweet.

Time slows until I can measure my heartbeats by the movements of my hands. And her breathing.

"What are you doing?" she says, barely above a whisper. There's no accusation in it, only wonder.

"Distracting you. I don't want you fainting on me." Although I'm also doing it for my own selfish reasons. Touching a woman has never felt this damn *good*. Warmth and pleasure and comfort flow from her skin to mine, soothing the last flickers of anger in me.

She's safe. The evidence is right there under my fingers.

"I don't feel faint." Her eyes are half-closed, her voice softer than I've ever heard from her.

"Good. But let's keep it up to be sure."

Her lips part, and I can sense her preparing one of her usual smart remarks. But it's a fight—she likes me touching her like this. And she doesn't want to stop me.

Interesting. If I weren't so entranced myself, I'd be thinking of ways to turn this to my advantage. Our *mutual* advantage, actually.

Instead, all I can do is keep massaging her wrists, letting this quiet, soft moment, so unlike any other between us, go on.

CHAPTER 6

Finn has me so distracted with the wrist massage I don't even notice where we've been driving until we pull up to his house.

"You live in Berkeley Hills?" I take in the woods surrounding the drive—his private drive—and the rolling hills around us. It's one of those "secrets of the East Bay"—Berkeley, home to a world-famous university and even more famous for its weirdos and hippies, has hills and woods and even deer roaming freely through the area. "You don't live in the City?"

He releases my wrists, and I bite back an instinctive protest. It felt… nice to have him do that. Really, really nice. And it didn't even seem like he was trying to seduce me.

"Nope. I like East Bay better." He gets out of the car, then gives me a hand out, all gentlemanlike. Which I already know he isn't, which makes the gesture that much more charming.

From the outside, his house looks like a particularly nice bungalow. The roof over the wraparound porch is supported by some columns, and the house is painted in tastefully cheery colors, blues and golds and dark green. The place is big by San Francisco standards, but it's definitely not a mansion.

Again, not what I was expecting from him. I pictured him in a modern, sleek house made of nothing but concrete and glass, right in the heart of the Marina district in the City. Basically, a charmless house in a neighborhood I hate, which is a complete one-eighty from this.

Then I walk inside and my breath is stolen away.

There doesn't seem to be a single wall within the place. I've stepped into an entirely open space—it's almost like the roof is floating above a huge row of picture windows that look out over the woods, the green of the trees tipped with gold in the late-evening light. And beyond that, the bay, with the bridge leading into San Francisco.

I feel like I can walk right out into that gorgeous scene before me.

The room is deliberately spare. There's some art on the walls—pen-and-ink sketches of desert scenes—and a collection of chairs scattered around a low table, all of them facing that amazing view. There's no dining table, no television, not even a sofa—nothing to sully the purity of the beauty just outside the windows.

Finn sees me taking it all in. "I like having space." He gestures to all the beautiful emptiness around us. "Helps me to think when there's no clutter."

Yes, this would be a great spot for some deep thinking. You could stare at the view, pace the entire length of the room, stare at the view some more… and then the solution to that knotty programming issue would appear.

I usually take a walk around the block when I get stuck on something. Sometimes I even run into someone who knew my brother and they ask how he's doing, when he'll get out. While I appreciate the concern and the knowledge that my brother isn't forgotten, walking around this room would be much, much nicer.

I realize then that there are no doors, at least none that I can see. "Where do you sleep?" I ask and immediately regret it.

Finn gives me a small, secret smile and pushes a panel next to a sketch of a Joshua tree. Part of the wall detaches and swings open, revealing a hidden door. "Back here. I figured it looked nicer without a door in the wall."

It does. In fact, it's delightful, and I can't help my silly smile.

But... it's also kind of mysterious. Actually, it's *very* mysterious. For all that he's friendly and a joker, he also seems to be carrying a lot of secrets.

I want to know more of those secrets, beyond what's behind this door. Which means I'll probably have to let him in on some of my secrets—and I already know that he plays for keeps.

He leads me into a hallway that looks sadly normal after the open space of the living room. There's an office, which looks as cluttered as I'd expect, and a bedroom with an unmade bed that makes me think dirty things and doing them with him in those rumpled sheets. My cheeks get uncomfortably hot, along with other, deeper parts of me.

This is definitely no guest room, kept pristine for whoever might drop by. This is his den, his lair, the intimate heart of him. This was the kind of secret I was hoping for, the kind that makes my heart beat faster.

Finn walks past the bed as if he doesn't even see it, leading me into his bathroom.

The disarray here is another sign of his ownership—there's a toothbrush only half put back in the holder, a tin of beard balm lying on the counter, the lid open, and some towels tossed over the shower door. It's luxurious but also lived-in.

Oh, and he gets naked in this room and rubs that big body of his down with soap, lets the water from the shower run over those massive muscles, then dries every inch of his skin.

My mouth is suddenly so dry it hurts. Even though the bathroom is huge, even by billionaire standards, it suddenly seems too small, Finn and my reaction to him taking up all the space.

He rummages through the medicine cabinet with easy unconcern though. And why not? This is his territory—he's in control here.

He begins to line up his instruments: tweezers, cotton swabs, rubbing alcohol, and a bunch of gauze.

"I really just need a Band-Aid." At least I think that's all I need. I don't want to look too closely at my hands and start feeling woozy again.

Just looking at Finn is making me woozy enough. I should just grab a Band-Aid and get out of here before I do something crazy, like kiss him. Or tear his clothes off.

I blink hard, but the images won't go away. I'm in shock. I have to be in shock, that's why I can't control my runaway fantasies.

"You need more than that," he rumbles. "Don't argue with me."

When he says it like that, some deep part of me doesn't want to. It wants to immediately do exactly what he asked.

I snap off a salute instead, reverting back to being a smart-ass. He rolls his eyes, then gestures for me to sit on the edge of the tub.

Calling it a tub is not giving this thing its full due though. It's marble, with swooping gold taps, deep enough to dive in, and with more jets than a hot tub.

We could have so much wet, slippery fun in that tub, Finn's hair and beard slicked down like a sexy seal as he dives under to kiss me—

"You going to sit?" he asks, raising an eyebrow.

I only just manage to hold back my squeak of shock. He didn't know what I was thinking, but I still feel like he's caught me with my hand in the cookie jar. "I'm taking in your tub. It's… something."

He laughs, low and knowing. "It is. Want to try it out?"

I fumble for a snappy answer, but my sarcasm generator seems to be malfunctioning. So I lift my palms. "Really, all I need is a Band-Aid." I sit down on the edge of the tub, ready to get this over with.

"Give me your hands." His voice is deep but gentle, reverberating through me.

I hold out the one that hurts the least. I turn my head, looking at the view of the hill behind us so I can't see what he's doing. There's probably blood, and I don't want to get woozy again.

But I can *feel* everything he's doing. His hand is warm, almost hot, his fingers long and thick as they cup my hands. On my palm, I feel gentle, brief swipes of a cotton ball, followed by a stinging coolness—he must be cleaning out my scrapes with rubbing alcohol. Which is overkill, but it's so sweet I'm touched in spite of myself.

Then he takes my thumb between his forefinger and his thumb and tilts it this way and that, as if transfixed by it. I can't see his expression, but my imagination fills in the blanks anyway. Maybe he's thinking about putting his lips against the soft pad of my thumb, his tongue darting out to taste my skin—

"Ouch!"

Pain stabs through my thumb. I try to jerk my hand back, but Finn's grip is too secure. My gaze snaps over to him instinctively, and I see him holding the tweezers, a massive splinter gripped in them. A massive splinter that used to be in my thumb.

Oh. My brain goes light, dizziness washing through me.

My thumb is still in his hand and I watch with horror as a bright red bead of blood wells up from the wound.

My cheeks go tingly, then cold, my stupid body betraying me at the sight.

It's only blood. Just a little dab of blood. Nothing to pass out over.

Which is what I always tell myself, but it doesn't work, like usual. My brain starts to feel fluttery and gray and…

And then Finn wraps his lips around my thumb. His tongue swipes across the pad, soothing my wound. He sucks once, twice, gently. His mouth is so warm it's almost hot, his tongue strong but soft. Velvety.

The dizziness is consumed by a rush of heat. I'm completely transfixed, so far from passing out I might never close my eyes again.

He pulls my thumb out of his mouth and studies it, his brow crinkling. It's like my thumb is as fascinating to him as he is to me. "I know you don't like the sight of blood."

His voice is as velvet soft as his tongue was. I should be feeling anything other than what I am right now. Shock or even indignation are the only appropriate responses. Not this lingering warmth in my heart, not the pulse of desire that pools between my legs, not my intense fascination with his mouth.

He could've used some gauze to wipe the blood—he *should* have used gauze—but now I can't imagine him using anything but his mouth to soothe all my hurts, even the invisible ones.

"Thanks," I say huskily. I don't pull out of his grip even though that would be the smart thing to do.

"Better?" His gaze is locked on mine so tight I can't see anything else.

I nod once, jerkily. My brain refuses to shift out of the slow, sensual gear he stuck it in.

He pulls a Band-Aid out of the box and wraps it around my thumb, then starts working on the rest of my scrapes. He's gentle about it, but I can't help my sharp inhales each time he touches a tender spot. Sadly, he doesn't use his tongue again.

"Sorry," he mutters, wincing with my every gasp. It's almost like this is hurting him more than it's hurting me.

I give his bent head a weak smile. There's no blood, but it does hurt, and that mixed with how close, how warm he is, is scrambling all of me. "It's really okay. You're much gentler than a doctor."

"Had a lot of practice," he says, giving a cut one last swab with the gauze, setting the gauze aside when he's done. "I've seen a lot of gnarly injuries on dirt bikes and ATVs."

"I don't think this quite qualifies as gnarly."

"No, it definitely does." The set of his mouth is grim, and I realize he's entirely serious. Somehow to him, my wounds are just as bad as the ones he seen on his big, tough, dirt-bike-riding friends.

He smears some antibiotic salve over the rest of my scrapes, then carefully binds them up with some gauze and tape. A few Band-Aids would've done just fine, but I get the sense he wants to be very thorough about this. So I let him; it's nice to be taken care of. When you live on your own, far away from your family, and are supposed to be an independent, can-do kind of woman, you can forget how nice these things feel.

As a final flourish, he hands me two ibuprofens and a glass of water.

"For the pain," he explains. "You're going to have a hell of a headache from the adrenaline shock."

He's right—there's the faint thrum of pain building behind my eyes. I obediently take the meds, then hand back the cup.

"I owe you now." Although I don't know what he could want from me. He's one of the richest men in America and one of the smartest. Yeah, he said he wanted to see my AI, but he's probably only insisting because I said no. He doesn't hear that word very often.

"Can I ask a favor then? Since I saved your life and all." His grin flashes, bright and surprising as a patch of sunlight in a storm cloud, and my heart does a flutter kick.

"Sure," I say without even thinking. Which is bad, because I need stay on my toes with this man. "What is it?" I force some suspicion into that to remind myself that he didn't get to where he is today by being soft and cuddly. Billionaires don't do soft and cuddly, especially not tech billionaires.

"I'd like to play a game of Go with you. Just you and me, face-to-face for once."

CHAPTER 7

We play out in his amazing living room, on a nineteen-by-nineteen board set up right next to the picture window. The board and the bowls of stones are sitting on a low table, the floor scattered with cushions. Clearly we're meant to sit cross-legged as we play.

I have to approve. Go isn't a game you should play while you're slumped in a chair. Your posture should be mindful, awake, meditative.

As a rule, Go boards aren't fancy, just a piece of smooth wood with a grid laid over it. And the markers are even less fancy—white and black stones, sleek and flat. The beauty of the board will appear in the patterns that form as we play.

The game pieces are collected into polished wooden bowls, designs inlaid in the wood. It's the only touch of embellishment, the designs reminding me of classic Go strategies.

I sink down onto one of the cushions, making sure that my back is straight and strong but not tense. I can see the campus from here, the campanile tall and bright as the setting sun hits it. Sunsets here must be amazing.

He sits with more grace than I'd expect, as big as he is. His posture mirrors mine—calm but alert. He gestures to the board with one broad hand. "As the guest, you get first choice of color."

My first instinct is to go for black. Black moves first, which gives it a strategic advantage. But I also don't want to seem like I need a handicap against him. We're evenly matched, and I don't want to win because of a tiny advantage. Hell, I want to win when I'm at a slight disadvantage. It will make victory all the sweeter.

"White." As I reach for the first stone, I catch myself. And not only because my hands flicker with pain thanks to my injuries. "Wait, are we playing for something?"

He raises an eyebrow as he reaches for his own game piece. "No. We're just playing. And talking."

"Oh." He's so competitive I don't know what to make of that. So I reach for my first piece and study the board, trying to decide how I'm going to annihilate him. Except I have to go slow, fishing a stone out of the bowls, my fingers clumsy and my palms wrapped tight in gauze. My heart zaps each time one of my scrapes tingles and I remember how gentle, how caring Finn was as he nursed me.

Finally I get a stone into my fingers and breathe through the erratic drumbeat of my pulse. Focus. I have to focus now.

We play the first twenty moves in absolute silence, the both of us considering how we're going to attack the other. I think I know what he's planning, and I've got a strategy to counter him, but he's surprised me before. I'm sure he'll do it now. We forget some of the more constraining etiquette rules, taking pieces before we've decided on a move and running them through our fingers as we ponder.

Formality has its place, but here it's just us. We don't need manners.

"When did you figure out it was me in the Go forums?" he asks out of the blue.

I study the board for a moment before I answer, "Actually, Anjie told me."

"Anjie?" He drops a stone back into the bowl with a clatter. "Why would she tell you that?"

"Because we talk. About stuff not related to work. I mentioned that I played Go. Then she mentioned that you also play Go and that you were pretty good at it. Her words, not mine," I clarify.

"Yeah, I figured that." He puts his chin in his hand as he studies the board, looking like some kind of philosopher/mountain-man/bad boy, thoughtful and bearded and muscular.

I silently clear my throat. "When you came into my Go forum, I slowly started to recognize your pattern of play. You know—smart but too dependent on being flashy when you need to get out of a bind."

His grin is rueful. "I didn't even guess it was you until the other night. Although I should've known—you took too much pleasure needling me during games."

"I never needled you." I start to place my piece, then think better of that move. It'll make my strategy too apparent. I need to be more subtle. "I was only playing the game."

He shakes his head. "There were definitely moments when you were mocking me with your moves. I could see it."

I want to argue with him, but maybe he's right. Certainly chasing him across the Go forums and setting my AI on him counts as needling him.

"What can I say?" I finally set down my marker, satisfied with my choice. The stone and my bandages flash bright white as the light catches on them. "You're so much fun to poke."

His answering smile is secret, sly, like I've just given everything away. He picks up his marker with deliberate slowness, using his thumb and forefinger and taking care not to rattle the stones in the bowl. His fingers are so massive the piece completely disappears between them. My mouth goes dry at the sight.

"When did you learn to play?" he asks softly.

I swallow, refocus my concentration on the board. "My brother taught me. He used to be really good actually, much better than I am."

His head jerks up. "Used to? Jesus, I'm so sorry."

His sympathy is expansive, open, so freely and quickly given I have to blink hard and look away.

"It's not like that," I explain quickly through the lump in my throat. "He's in prison."

"I'm sorry," he says again. There's no surprise or censure in his voice.

"It wasn't his fault." I'm defensive even though Finn isn't judgmental.

I take a deep breath. I want to tell him about Ray, explain all of it, but it hurts to talk about it. People aren't exactly mean when I tell them, and it's not a secret, but everyone's uncomfortable after. They try to be enlightened, but my brother has a serious mental illness and is in prison—people instinctively react like it's contagious.

But I'm not ashamed of Ray. I still love him. I want Finn to understand that, to see my brother beyond his illness and his conviction.

"I say brother, but he's my twin." I keep my eyes on the game board, twisting a stone through my fingers. My injuries protest, but I keep going. The pain helps me focus. "He was in grad school at Berkeley when he started to develop schizophrenia."

Finn makes a low noise of sympathy and encouragement.

"He tried all kinds of medication, but the side effects were awful. Almost worse than the symptoms. Eventually he ended up on the streets in a particular neighborhood in Oakland. I moved there to be close to him, and tons of other people in the neighborhood kept an eye on him. It wasn't ideal, not at all, but it could have been much worse."

"What happened then?" His voice is deep and soft, comforting.

"There was a robbery at the local drugstore. A big one. The police claimed they had him on camera doing it. The cashier said it wasn't him—he was a regular there, all the employees knew him—but that didn't matter to the jury. They convicted Ray anyway."

There's a long silence, broken only by our breathing. Finn is looking at me, steady, calm, and completely open. He almost looks more vulnerable than I feel, but he's so big it doesn't quite get there. Instead, it makes me think of safety. Of refuge.

"So he's better than you?" Finn finally asks, gesturing at the board. "I'll have to play him someday, just to get a real challenge."

I stiffen. What the heck does he mean, *a real challenge?*

Then his smile comes on, slow and sticky, and I realize that he's teasing me. And I feel at ease again.

"I'll show you a real challenge," I say, jutting my chin out.

"I'll bet you will."

I shiver at the implications of that, because I know he's talking about more than simply our game here.

He sets down his piece, then leans back to study the board. "So, tell me more about him. Is he as ornery as you?"

I frown at the game before I answer. Dammit, he's not doing what I thought he would. This is some new, unpredictable strategy of his. "Ray's not ornery exactly. But he's super sarcastic. People can think he's mean because his sense of humor is so dry, but he's really not. I mean, he fosters stray cats. Or at least he used to."

That had been the hardest thing for him when he became homeless, losing his foster kitties. He adopted some street cats, but they were more independent than his foster cats. He didn't get the love he needed from them.

I set my piece down, keeping to my original strategy even

though Finn's changed his. He might be getting erratic simply to throw me off.

"You strike me as a cat person," Finn says. He makes his move immediately, again with no discernible method to his madness.

"Oh no, I'm totally a dog person." I nibble on my lower lip, trying to decipher what he's doing. Should I change my plan of attack?

It's so much harder to concentrate with him right next to me. I'm horribly aware of him just existing, big and brash and taking up so much space. Even his breathing can't be ignored. I know he's not doing it on purpose, but I'm almost as focused on him as I am on the game.

What were we talking about?

"Um, yeah, I like dogs better." I tap a stone against my lips, then catch myself. I can't give anything away to him. "They're so much more lovable. Always happy to see you, always wanting to be with you... It's nice to be loved that unconditionally."

My face gets hot as I realize that I've just given way more away than a simple observation. It sounds like I'm lonely or something. Which I'm not.

Suddenly my eyes start burning, because yes, I very much am. I've got my family and January and everyone else at Ultra, but it's still been so hard. My parents are terrified about Ray, have been for years, and while I am too, I've got to be upbeat and strong for them. I've got to believe hard enough for all of us.

And my friends... They're supportive, of course they are. But they don't carry this burden twenty-four seven like I do. Talking with them helps, but at the end of the day, it's just me and my worries.

So yes, I'm lonely. Very much so.

"A dog would be nice," I finish weakly. "But since I work

so much and can't have a pet in my apartment, it's not possible."

"Yeah." His voice is low, meant only for me. "A dog would be nice."

He's richer than sin, but he can't have a dog. That's like the saddest thing I've ever heard.

Finn sets down his marker, then leans back and crosses his arms. The massiveness of them catches me up short every time.

And then I look back at the board, my mouth dropping open. "What the…?"

He's done it again, that crazy, erratic, out-of-nowhere brilliance, coming up on my blind side and defeating me. There's no way for me to win. I have to resign.

Etiquette demands I play a few more moves, not resign too quickly. Let my emotions cool so I don't come off as a sore loser.

But there's no way my emotions can ever cool being this close to Finn. "I resign," I say with little grace, setting two stones on the board to make my surrender that much clearer.

I told him all that stuff about my brother, and he didn't let me win.

My mouth spreads in a wide smile. He gave me comfort but not pity. Which is the happiest—and sexiest—thing I can think of. Clearly he was affected by my brother's story, but he respected me enough to play his very best.

Maybe I should give him my AI code. Or sleep with him. Or both.

But first our match isn't finished and I've got some games to win. We keep quiet during this one, focused solely on the game. We're both in beast mode now.

Only, I can't stop thinking about him. Every time I catch sight of my hands, the bandages bright white and my palms aching, I remember his head bent over me, his gentle care as he nursed me back to health. And then, worst of all, his mouth on my thumb.

Somehow though, I take the second game, more through his mistakes than through my own prowess. It doesn't matter —a victory is a victory.

He resigns the game without a word, placing a captured stone on the board to signal his loss. Beneath his beard, I can see his jaw tensing—he does not like to lose.

The sight makes me think of his jaw moving in other situations. Like when he might be kissing someone—okay, *me*—and how his beard might feel against my skin when he did.

"Best of three?" The request rumbles out from deep in his chest. It vibrates through my hands and up my arms, and I have to hold in my shiver.

"Sure." I go for white again.

Something shifts between us this time, heavily uncurling over the board. The first game, I opened up to him, told him about my brother, and he offered his sympathy, his comfort. The second game was all-out competition.

This game is different. I move like I'm trapped underwater, my limbs slow and weighted. Or at least it feels like that. I'm hyperaware of everything Finn does, even when it's nothing at all.

He's as focused on me as I am on him. Half the time he's looking at my mouth or my hair or my breasts instead of the board. But he still plays like a fiend, unthinking brilliance flashing from some of his moves. And he doesn't even have to ponder them—the move leaps into his mind and in the next second into his fingers.

His fingers… They're thick and surprisingly long, and the way they move over the stones has me imagining how they'd move over my pussy, my clit. I'm on fire, my body dragging me toward thoughts of beds and hard, fast sex and my mind clinging to thoughts of strategies and moves.

"Hmm," Finn says as I take my turn, setting up a trap that ought to snap on him in about ten moves. "Interesting."

My toes curl because he says it so... *so knowingly*. He looks me up and down, his gaze hot and a touch possessive, just so I get the point. This is a game *and* a seduction. Or foreplay. Or both.

I give him a cat's grin. "Isn't it?" I reach for my next piece, taking the time to let my fingertips linger over the smooth stone. "Let's see if you figure out what I'm up to."

One of his eyebrows lifts, just a touch. "Oh, I think I'm learning you inside and out."

I catch my exhale before I embarrass myself. "Make your move."

His hand hovers over the board, which is terribly rude, but then the rules never anticipated Go as foreplay. "Here?" He looks to a square, then looks back at me, dark mischief in his expression. "Or here?" He looks at my neck, right where my pulse is fluttering against my skin.

"You could try there," I purr. "See where it gets you."

"Maybe not there." His hand moves to a different square while his gaze moves lower, right where my shirt opens to reveal the swell of my breasts. "Here looks better."

My breasts tighten as if his hand is squeezing them and not the game piece. My nipples drag against the lace of my bra, and I know, know deep in my core, he can see and he loves it.

"Maybe," I say, only a little breathless. "I don't know what your strategy is."

"Still haven't figured it out yet?" He tsks as he shakes his head. "It looks pretty clear from here." His gaze flicks from one of my nipples to the other, as hot and intense as anything.

He sets down his stone with a soft click that throbs through me. I bite the inside of my lower lip, letting that small pain anchor me.

Do I want to win this game, or do I want to be seduced? My brain is telling me to win while my body is screaming for seduction.

Finn is hot and brilliant and rich. If I resign the game now, we can be in his bed in under five seconds.

But if I slip into his bed, it won't be a one-night thing. Once I get a taste of Finn, I'm going to want more and more and more. And really, my life just doesn't have room for *more*. With Ray and my job and my AI, I barely have time to sleep.

I might be lonely and exhausted and desperate for someone, anyone, to help with my brother's situation, but Finn isn't the person to fill the hole in my life even if I was looking for someone to do that. He's only looking for someone to play with here.

So even though my body is throwing a five-alarm tantrum, I take several slow, deep breaths, refocusing on the game board. I see suddenly what he has planned and how my trap for him will snap shut in eight moves, not ten. As long as I focus and stick to my strategy.

Which I do, making my next few moves with ice-cold precision. In seven moves, he leans back from the board, his expression shuttered.

He knows he's lost more than the game here.

"I resign," he says, low and gravelly. But there's a challenge there.

You've won this one. But we'll play again.

"I should go home," I say, not even acknowledging his words. Because even though I've won this game, if I stay, I'll lose even more.

CHAPTER 8

I don't know what the fuck just happened back at my place, and I'm not very happy about it. When I lose, I want to know why.

I definitely had Doc with me at first, flushed and ripe and *this close* to falling into my arms. Then somewhere my strategy went sideways. I lost both the game and her, although I didn't give a damn about the game.

She's not even looking at me as she sits in the passenger seat of my Tesla. I can't imagine the sights of downtown Oakland are that exciting, especially since she's seen them before.

When she said she had to go—when she shut down completely on me—I didn't argue. I asked where she lived, then pulled the Tesla out of the garage. I'm driving all nice and sweet, partly to hold back my foul mood and partly to stick it to Doc.

Want a nice guy? I can be nice.

Except I can't, and it's not because I'm a bastard that she pulled away. It was something else entirely.

I've never been able to resist a puzzle, and Doc is the sexiest, most compelling puzzle I've ever met.

"How are your hands?" I ask. Every splinter, every bit of

gravel I dug out of her palms was a dart straight to my heart. I can't stop thinking about her flinches, the tears in her soft skin.

And how she tasted when I took her thumb in my mouth. Salty but sweet, pure enticement with a thread of copper.

"They'll be okay." Finally she forces her gaze over to me. "Thank you for what you did. All of it."

The gratitude in her voice makes me want her to say that again, only this time about something much better. Like an orgasm or two.

"Make sure to put antibacterial cream on it." My hands go tight around the steering wheel, as tight as my groin is. "If it looks infected, get to a doctor ASAP. I'll pay for it."

"Didn't you tell me you've broken a ton of bones?" she asks dryly. "And you're freaking out over some scrapes?"

"When they're yours, yes."

Her blush looks good enough to eat. I bet her pussy goes that exact shade of pink when she gets aroused. I bet it was that exact color—maybe even deeper—when we were playing that last game.

I smash down on the brake pedal, just missing the green light. If she hadn't been with me, I would have floored it and taken my chances.

See how nice I can be? Even though I fucking hate *nice.*

"It's just around the corner here," she says, even though the car navigation said that already.

I nod at the construction site across the street. "Didn't that used to be a diner?"

"Yeah." She starts to put her chin in her hand, then catches herself, staring at her bandages. Once more, I resolve to tear the Oakland police chief a new one. "I guess it had been there for forty years. But a developer wanted to build some high-rise apartments, and he made them an offer they couldn't turn down. The same company is putting up another high-rise a block over."

"Gordian Development," I read off the sign in front. The artist's illustration of the high-rise looks completely fucking charmless, as sterile as every other high-rise going up across the bay in the City.

Give these developers enough time, and they'll turn Oakland into a clone of SoMa in San Francisco, choked with office buildings and coders and utterly without character, which is a damn shame. Oakland is often overshadowed by the City, but in its own way it's got more personality than San Francisco.

Doc sighs, a sound so sad I immediately want to make her feel better, make her laugh, smile, toss some snark at me. "We tried to stop at least one of the high-rises, but no luck."

The light changes and I hit the accelerator. The Tesla surges forward. I want to stop those high-rises for her, but even if I could, there's no bringing back the diner. I can't turn back time, not even for her.

I frown. Now that's a weird thought.

There's a little noise from her, half gasp, half sob, but so quiet I almost miss it.

"Doc, are you…?"

When I see what she's looking at, I don't have to finish that question. It's a drugstore, a chain that's on every other corner in the Bay Area. Nothing special about it, but I immediately know that's the drugstore her brother supposedly robbed.

I don't know if he's innocent, but I know Doc is hurting right now.

"Shit, I had no idea." I search for a place to turn. But there's nothing—we'll have to go right by it. "I'm sorry."

"It's okay." Her gaze is tight on the drugstore as it slides past the car window. "Sometimes I take another route to avoid it. And other days I make myself go by, just to remind myself. To remember."

"How much have you spent on legal fees?" I ask. She

didn't specifically say so, but I can hear it in her voice—she's poured too much into her brother's case. Of course that's going to include money along with her energy.

She laughs humorlessly. "Enough so that I don't have a safety net. Enough so that I'm living paycheck to paycheck."

The drugstore disappears behind us. I take one last look in the rearview mirror, and my memory clicks, slides into place.

I've seen this before, this exact drugstore, this exact intersection. Except where?

I might be a genius, but I don't have a photographic memory. If I did, I would have done a damn sight better in school. I let the back part of my brain chew on it as I finish driving to her apartment building.

"That was Ray's spot." Her voice is carefully neutral as she points out a grassy patch in a postage-stamp-sized park. There are a few people camped there.

Her apartment is literally around the corner. She must have seen her brother every day.

"So you were pretty close then," I say, keeping my voice just as neutral. I wonder how much of this January knows. How much anyone else in Doc's life does.

"Yeah." She looks at her hands in her lap, wrapped in gauze. "I tried so many times to get him into housing, get him back into treatment… I even offered him the floor of my room, which my roommates would've hated. Nothing convinced him."

"It's not your fault." Her guilt tears at me. Which confuses me. I've been with plenty of women but feeling guilty with them? Wanting to make over their lives so they're utterly perfect? That's not me.

I'm the clown. With women I laugh, I have fun, and then I move on. I don't fix shit for them.

I want to fix everything for Doc, and I can't. Which makes me as furious as a caged lion.

"It's not about fault," she says with a long sigh. "I know it's all up to him, and he's fighting this terrible, awful disease, but… He failed and I failed. And if ever get him home, I need to figure out how not to fail again."

Holy shit, this is heavy. I've got a few friends who've done time, all for stupid shit like DUIs and growing weed or cooking meth. Which isn't to say I'm an angel, but when you get to where I am in the food chain, crimes don't send you to jail. You get a slap on the wrist, a fine that's less than your daily income, and we're all friends again. I'd have to do something spectacular to get sent to prison, like swindling rich people out of a lot of their money.

Which is why I don't flaunt what I do have. I'm not going to brag or rub it in, because I'm not any better than those guys I left behind in Rancho Carne.

"I'll help you," I say. And I mean it.

She slants me a look. A suspicious look. "I don't want to owe you anything. I can't owe you anything—I already owe too much to other people."

My jaw goes tight, but I hold back the rest of my reaction. I wasn't offering so she could owe me. My helping her with her brother and us figuring out this attraction between us would be two separate things.

"It wouldn't be like that," I get out. Turning me down flat like that is silly, and Doc's not silly. Money can solve pretty much anything—look at what I've done with my hometown.

I whip into a parking spot right in front of her building, forgetting to drive nice. She grabs the door handle, her eyes going wide, her lips wet and parted.

"Ooh." Her hand tightens on the handle. "You slipped into that quick."

Okay, if she's going to set up hits like that, I have to take a swing. It's instinct with me. "Yeah, but I like to take my time when I get there."

I can't tell if she wants to roll her eyes or smile. I'll take both, because it means she's cheering up.

And I'm going to look into her brother's case anyway, without telling her. Something about that drugstore is familiar, but my brain still hasn't pulled up what it is. I need some time in the secure facility, going through files to find it. But it's there.

"What, all of thirty seconds?" she asks, one eyebrow raised.

"Yep, thirty seconds to your first orgasm. We'd go slow with the second one. Third could be fast again. Or slow. Lady's choice."

Okay, now she's rolling her eyes *and* smiling, which is a great look on her. Sassy, smart women have always been my kryptonite.

"You're a big talker." Her hand's on the door latch, but she's not opening it. In fact, she's fully turned toward me, her eyes sparkling.

"I'm a hell of a lot more than talk."

The spark in her eyes flares. "I'd bet not." But her voice is shaky with uncertainty and desire.

"You don't want to find out 'cause I'd prove you wrong." God, never have I wanted so badly to prove her wrong, to take her mouth and win her. Win her over.

Her swallow is long and slow, and my gaze is stuck to the elegant column of her throat. My tongue tingles as I imagine tasting that soft skin of hers.

"No, you won't."

"I'll make it good. Better than you've ever had. And you know it."

"There's no room in my life for complications right now."

"It won't be complicated. Not at all. It'll be the easiest thing in the world. Just let me take charge."

She sighs like that's the best thing she's heard in a long time, like she's ready to slip into my arms and never leave.

She closes her eyes, one corner of her mouth ticking up. "I don't know."

When she opens her eyes again, they're haunted. My every instinct—protective, aggressive, comforting—comes roaring to life. I put a hand to her jaw, breathe her in, savor the leap of her pulse, hammering at the base of her neck.

"Let me give you the answer then." I lower my mouth to hers, and I'm so desperate to taste her it feels like it takes years before our lips meet.

Her mouth is cool at first, like the early-morning touch of fog. Her lips part under mine, and she does that sigh again, like this is the best thing she's experienced in a long time. That sigh strokes down my cock, tightens my thighs.

I should take my time, give her space to ease into this, but that's never been my style. Going zero to sixty is more fun the faster you do it.

I nudge open her mouth, slide my tongue along her lips. She tastes like heat and need and a touch of cinnamon. My lungs hitch because I've never had a kiss that tasted this damn *right*.

Her head falls back, a silent admission that she's loving this, that she's ready to get lost in this kiss. I tuck a hand in the small of her back and lift her toward me, pulling her against me. Her hand finds my shoulder and twists in the fabric of my shirt, fiercely anchoring me to her. Fuck, but that's hot.

"I'm not going anywhere." I nip at her lower lip, because it's so pouty it's begging to be bitten.

"Less talking. More kissing."

I want to laugh and kiss her senseless at the same time. Goddamn, but she really is perfect. I do as she says, using my tongue to taste every inch of her mouth. When her tongue meets mine, it's like stars or fireworks or I don't even know, because it's too fucking mind-blowing for words. Her glasses press against the edge of my nose, dig into my cheek, which somehow drives me even wilder.

I've never fucked a woman in the front seat of a car—the back seat, sure, plenty of times—but I'm about five seconds away from doing exactly that with Doc. And all because of a kiss.

We're breathing hard between kisses, gasping for air in bursts before we dive back into each other. Why do we have to breathe again? Why can't I keep my mouth on hers forever?

Because this woman is special. I want to take my time, make it mind-blowing for the both of us, not grope blindly in the front seat of my car.

Inch by agonizing inch, I pull away from her. She tries to follow, her eyes closed, her lips kiss stung, her hair looking like the morning after.

Fuck. I wish I were a bigger dirtbag so I could keep kissing her.

When she opens her eyes, I see sanity come rushing back. Her tongue comes out to wet her lips—which, seriously, is she trying to kill me?—and she pushes her hair behind her ears, the purple waves springing back the second she lets go.

We stare at each other for a long moment, and I swear I can hear her heartbeat, soft and insistent.

"I..." She gestures behind her at her building. "I have to go." But she doesn't open the door.

Which leaves me another perfect opening. In an instant I'm out of the car and opening the door for her, offering my hand. I've helped women out of cars before, but I've never meant it like I do now.

Doc takes a moment to adjust her glasses and smooth her hair, taking a deep inhale when she's done. But her cheeks are still pink and her lips... Her lips are going to carry my mark for hours.

She lifts her chin as she puts her hand in mine, the

bandages scratchy. "You didn't win," she says, back to her usual defiance. "That was definitely a draw."

"A draw?" I splutter as I pull her into my body. "The hell it was."

She pointedly looks down at the erection that's not at all hidden in my jeans. Then she looks up and raises one eyebrow.

My cock jumps.

She smiles.

I smile back, leaning in to whisper in her ear. "I'll take a draw then. Because that means there's going to be a rematch."

CHAPTER 9

I stumble into work next morning feeling like I've been hit
by a BART train. My knee throbs, my hands ache, and my
scrapes sting. And I'm tired as hell since I spent most of the
night awake and thinking of Finn.

"You okay?" January asks the minute I step through the
doors. I must look terrible to have her looking so concerned
the moment she sees me.

"I'm fine. Just tired." I reach for the cross-body strap on
my bag and wince. "Okay, maybe a little banged up too."

"Banged up?" January rises from behind her desk. "What
happened?"

It's only the two of us here, and since it's a Saturday, I was
kind of hoping no one would be around. I mean, I love
January, but I need some quiet time after yesterday.

"I went to the protest last night."

"Oh my God." January puts her hand to her throat, then
rushes over to me. "You were in the middle of that?"

"I'm amazed you know about it." I drop my bag on my
chair, gasping when the strap leaves my hands. Damn, but
those scrapes hurt even after Finn's tender loving care.

"I should've known you'd be there." January clucks at me
as she takes in my bandaged hands. "I don't mean this in a

mean way, but is this really helping Ray? He wouldn't want you to get hurt."

I catch myself before I get defensive, because January is simply worried about me. "I have to do something beyond paying ridiculous legal fees. I'm surprised you even heard about the protest. The media was there, but they usually ignore us."

January hands me some water and ibuprofen. "They said something about scuffles as the news conference broke up. I could read between the lines."

I swallow the pills gratefully. I was out at my house, and I refuse to go to the nearest drugstore for obvious reasons. "Yeah, we all got caught in those lines. Specifically, between a line of riot cops and a line of barricades."

January hovers her hands over my elbow, which is nicely purple. She frowns like she wants to do something but has no idea what.

"Really, it looks worse than it is." I clear my throat, my cheeks going warm. "Finn was there. He, uh… helped me?"

That came out way squeakier than I wanted.

January raises an eyebrow. "Helped?"

I plop myself in my chair like a sullen teen. "Okay, he technically, kind of, rescued me."

January purses her lips in a silent whistle. "Mark's Finn? Rescued you?"

I know for a fact that Finn would never describe himself as Mark's Finn. He's his own person, the most his own person I've ever met.

"He doesn't really belong to Mark, does he?"

January raises her eyebrows. "I thought you didn't like him?"

Man, that's a tough one. Because of course I like him. He's funny, he's brilliant, and he's mega-mega-hot. Like, I'm ready to melt into slag around him hot.

Okay, I *did* melt into slag when I kissed him. If he hadn't pulled away first...

But he's also infuriating and way too full of himself, and I've got more than enough drama and trouble in my life. He might be hot, but he's also capital *T* trouble.

"He's fine," I say quickly. "The cops were coming after us, batons raised, and everyone panicked. Like, bolted, stampeded. And I was about to fall down. He caught me."

My heart catches as I remember the panic of falling, then his strong arms around me, never letting go. And his head bent over my hands as he cleaned my wounds. And his mouth as it reduced me to a quivering mass right on my front doorstep.

"Oh." January's eyes widen as she ponders that. "That's kind of romantic."

"Yeah, except for the massive police presence and the hundreds of people they were threatening to beat down," I say cheerily.

January smiles. "Well, of course. Take away the riot police though, and it's pretty much a fairy tale. Why was Finn at the protest? Besides to rescue you?"

"Keeping an eye on Fuchs. Minerva was there."

January's mouth twists like she just bit into a lemon. The mention of Minerva Dyne tends to have that effect on people. "Oh, that..." January can't think of a word bad enough to call her.

I can think of a few, but I keep them to myself. "Yep, our favorite person. But we knew Corvus was working on this surveillance project."

"He's like a bad penny. He always turns up."

"What exactly is a bad penny?" I ask. "I mean, who even uses pennies anymore?"

"Maybe it's more like Canadian pennies. You think, 'Oh, I have just enough change to get that candy bar,' but then no—

it was actually a Canadian coin all along. And you've tossed out that same Canadian coin a dozen times."

"Calling Arne Fuchs Canadian is a big insult to Canada though."

"True." January shakes her head. "Wait, you're distracting me. We were talking about Finn. And how he saved you."

I blink at her. "Wow. You just put way too many syllables into saved."

"It's exciting. It needs extra syllables to get all the excitement across." January tilts her head. "Should I sing it instead? That would also be exciting."

I throw my head back and laugh, then grab my elbow and grimace. How the heck would laughing make my elbow hurt? "Please, no singing. It really wasn't that exciting."

January simply stares at me.

I sigh. "Okay, it was." I put my hands between my knees and lean close. "He took me back to his house to bandage me up. Have you ever seen that place? It's amazing."

January shakes her head. "We've only been to Logan's—I figured Finn's house wasn't big enough for all of us. I'm sure he's got a room-sized gaming rig or something."

"Um…" I catch myself, because I did see his gaming rig, and I'm guessing he hasn't let many people see that. "His house is pretty big. And it's built for…" I search for the right word. Not entertaining and not relaxing… "For thinking. Deep thinking."

"I can't tell if you're infatuated with him or his house."

"Neither." I rear back, away from her insights. "He's got a nice house; he clearly wants people to comment on it."

"And yet I've never been there." January crosses her arms. "But you have."

"Because I was bleeding." Although not that much. He could have taken me home. I could have insisted he take me home. But I didn't.

"And he rescued you," January says, determined not to let this go.

I lift my palms and exhale in exasperation. "Okay, fine. I'm really attracted to him. Happy now?" I spit that out because I'm still kind of mad at my body for that. This really isn't the time for me to be falling for a billionaire bad boy. "I could list all the reasons why, but you already know them. Problem is, he's our funder. And my life is already a mess. He'd be like a bull, and my china shop is already kind of busted up."

January huffs in indignation. "Your china shop is not busted up. It's beautiful."

Thank God for friends like January. I don't think I'd have survived the past year without her. "You're sweet to say that. But I'm walking through broken glass here. I've got to concentrate on not stepping on any shards."

"You could let Finn carry you."

"I think we've let this metaphor get way out of hand." I pull out my laptop and fire it up.

But January sees through my bluff. "Wait, did you tell Finn about your... china shop?"

I stare at my home screen, my eyes stinging. I try to put my fingers on the keys, but the aches in my palms remind me of everything that happened yesterday. Everything that I can't run away from.

"I told him everything," I tell January quietly. "And then I let him kiss me."

Her gasp is incredibly loud in the empty office. "Was he weird about it?"

I shake my head. "He was actually great. He asked me about Ray, about how he was before he got sick. Nobody ever does that." I clench my jaw and breathe hard through my nose. "He also offered to help with Ray's case. I turned him down, which was probably stupid."

January rubs my shoulder, pushing comfort and strength

into me. "Hey, it's a lot to tell anyone about what happened to Ray. It's totally understandable you wouldn't immediately jump on his offer to help."

"But I need all the help I can get." I look up at January, imploring her to understand. "Except I don't want to owe him. I don't want to put Finn in the same pile as all the lawyer bills and the expert witnesses and the psychiatrists."

"Of course you don't. You've done so much for Ray. You need something for yourself."

I rub my eyes, trying to get control of my emotions. "I've got my job. And my AI."

January snorts. "Every woman needs more than that. You're allowed to get some hot sex too."

I giggle so loud I scare myself. "He really is something, isn't he?" I can feel my expression going dreamy as I remember everything about Finn. His big, hard body. His tender care. His fucking amazing brain.

"Um…" January assumes a diplomatic expression. "He's not quite my type, but yeah."

I roll my eyes. "You wouldn't have said that before you met Mark. I swear, you two can only see each other. Speaking of, where is he? Why are you working on a Saturday?"

Weekends are exclusively Mark and January time. January used to work eighty-hour weeks, and then she got together with Mark and suddenly she disappeared on the weekends. Which I totally approve of.

"Oh, somebody they invested in is running his start-up into the ground, so Mark called him in this weekend to read him the riot act. I figured I could get caught up here while he played the hard-ass at work." She looks around the office, her expression wistful. "Not that there's much for me to clean up with you running the team."

"Do you want me to start screwing up so you'll have more to do? Because I can."

She shakes her head. "Impossible. But it's awesome you came in—we can play weekend catch-up together, just like we used to. Should we order in from that Nepalese place for lunch?"

My mouth waters. "You read my mind. But first..." I wake up my laptop. "We should probably do some work."

January settles into her own desk as I call up my code. But as I do, the secure app we use here at Ultra, the one January coded herself, pings that I have a message. It's probably Valentina, telling me about the most recent tests she ran on the latest encryption algorithm.

Except it's not. "Who the hell is SlowGold?" I squint at my screen and adjust my glasses as if that will give me the answer. "January, I think someone hacked your messaging app."

She's up in an instant and coming around to see my screen. I lean to one side so that she can see better. "That's almost impossible. That app is encrypted harder than the NSA." She frowns at the message, then pulls up the guts of the code, shuffling through it. "Huh."

I look myself, but I can't see what's so interesting. If there's something I should be recognizing in there, I'm not.

January types some more on my keyboard, then grins at me. "Finn sent this."

"What?" I look back at the screen. "How do you know?"

"This was sent from the Bastard Capital office. I know because Mark sends me messages from this address all the time." Her grin flattens. "I guess Finn was able to hack my program."

"Or Mark gave him access." I call up the message proper. "SlowGold..." I roll my eyes as I realize the significance, feeling stupid. I'm QuikSilver on the Go boards, so he's SlowGold here. Of course. "Yep, it's definitely Finn."

"What did he send you?" January asks in a singsong voice. "Maybe he's asking you out."

I kind of doubt Finn does anything so boring as dating. "Let's see."

When I open the message, a dozen images pop up. They're all grayscale, grainy—images from a security camera. My brain whirrs as I try to match the images with something, anything I know.

"Oh God." I put my knuckles to my teeth and bite, hard. "Oh my God."

"Ramona." January is freaked out—she never uses my given name, and she never lets her voice crack like that. "What is it?"

I click through the photos one more time, just to make sure I'm seeing what I am. "That's Ray." I point to a blurry figure walking on the sidewalk in one of the shots, the infamous drugstore in the background. "He's got one of his cats under his arm."

I can't tell from the picture, but that must be Opus—his other cats wouldn't have let him carry them like that. Opus needs wet food since his teeth are so bad, and Ray made sure he always had it.

I buy the wet food for Opus now and give it to Kevin, one of Ray's friends who adopted Opus when Ray left. I tried to keep Opus myself, but he just kept running away. You know, like a big fat metaphor for my relationship with my brother.

"Are these pictures from the trial?" January asks.

I shake my head. I looked at the evidence photos forward and backward and sideways, trying to find anything that would let my brother go free. I never found it.

"Those photos were from cameras inside the store and one in the parking lot." I point to a speck high on a light pole. "That's the parking lot camera. I have no idea what camera took these." I flip through the rest of the pictures, which are all of Ray but in different parts of our neighborhood, all taken with different surveillance cameras. "And look: they're time-stamped… These were all taken on different dates at different times."

I sit back hard in my chair, my lungs flattening. Someone was stalking my brother. And doing it with some pretty sophisticated cameras.

"Are those Oakland PD cameras?" January asks. "Where did Finn get those?"

"They shouldn't be from the Oakland PD," I say heavily. "Their panopticon isn't supposed to have started yet. They can't be using surveillance cameras, not if they're telling the truth."

As for where Finn got them… The genius hacker must have broken into some system locked up tighter than Fort Knox to get these. I have a pretty good idea which system that was.

"Corvus," January and I say together.

We share a long look, brimming with shared under-standing.

"If he really hacked them…," she starts.

"…it's unbelievable," I finish. "That's like an Olympic-level hack."

My fingers tingle as I look at the photos again, but not because of my injuries. If he's found these, maybe he has the key to Ray's innocence. Maybe Finn really can help me.

"You have to go talk to him," January says. "Right now."

The message app pings again. *Rematch?*

I grab my bag, not even caring that my hands hurt like hell. "Yep. And I know exactly where he is."

CHAPTER 10

I look up at the clock on the wall, watching as the second hand sweeps around, counting down to when the minute hand can click over. If my calculations are correct—and they always are—Doc should be arriving...

"Where did you get those pictures?" The question bursts out of her as loudly as the door slams against the wall. Her eyes are wide and wild behind her glasses, and her hair looks like I've run my hands through it. Her mouth, sadly, looks very unkissed. I'll have to do something about that.

Two minutes for her to tear out of the Ultra offices when she got my message, five minutes to get onto the 280, thirty-eight minutes to get to the off-ramp for the secure facility, then another three minutes to get to our parking lot, and I gave her thirty seconds to climb out of her car and march in here.

I got it to the exact minute. I smile to myself. Shit, but I'm good.

"Why are you smiling?" Her mouth is tight, her finger pointing at me. "How did you hack Corvus?"

I drop my amusement. "Corvus? I didn't hack them. Those pictures were from an Oakland PD server. Some moron left his password as password1234."

She slumps so hard I worry she'll pass out. Once more, I'm jumping over my desk, grabbing her before she hits the floor.

"I'm okay," she says dryly as she looks up at me. But she's not pushing me off, and she's softer than she looks, her curves sweeter for being on the more discreet side.

"You sure? It seemed like you'd seen some blood."

Heat pulses between us as we both remember her thumb in my mouth, the sweet salt of her taste spreading over my tongue.

"No blood," she says, soft as her curves.

"I can check. Just to be sure." My pulse throbs, hard and insistent.

She does that sigh, that one that taps right into the animal in me, then pushes against my shoulder. Weakly though. I'm guessing it's not only because her hand is hurt.

"We need to discuss these pictures," she says. "And where you got them."

I set her down, making sure she slides against me as I do. "Did you change the bandages today? How does it look? Do you need a doctor?"

Her cheeks go the most adorable shade of pink. Shy pink, I'd call that, which contrasts nicely with her bold purple hair. "Um, yes. No. I mean, yes, I changed the bandages. And no, I don't need a doctor."

"Good. I can still take a look."

She bites her lip. Then she blinks. "The pictures? You didn't get them from Corvus?"

Right. The other thing I want to show her. "Not even I can hack Corvus, at least not from the outside."

She frowns at the word "outside" but doesn't get caught up on it. "But the police aren't supposed to be recording. Not yet."

I lead her over to my workstation, pulling out the chair

and guiding her into it. "I don't think those pictures came from police cameras." I reach over her to start typing.

She slides me a look from under her lashes, which is so fucking enticing. "There isn't another chair you can use?"

"Nope. I'll just type over you." And enjoy the scent of her shampoo.

She gives a pointed look at the many chairs around us. I smile back with all the innocence I can summon.

"Go ahead," she says, half-amused, half-annoyed.

"Okay." I type out commands, pulling up the files I have, my focus completely on that. Okay, mostly on that. "I decided to go poking into the Oakland PD servers."

"When?"

"A while back," I answer coolly. I'm not going to tell her exactly when it happened because it's not important. "After your brother's trial but before the Corvus/Oakland PD panopticon announcement."

"Are you not telling me exactly when to protect me or you?"

"Both." I pop my jaw as I finish calling up the images. "Hackers who brag about their hacks get caught. I haven't been caught yet, and I'm not going to."

I've got enough money to buy my way out of any problem, but that's not the point. I love looking into places where I'm not supposed to be and doing it undetected. It gives me a high that not even money does.

I mean, money is too easy. Hacking is still hard. After growing up dirt-poor with way too much energy and brains, I got a taste for hard. Which is difficult to find these days, considering how successful I am.

Doc gives me that same thrill that hacking does though. Maybe even a bigger one.

So yeah, I'm still addicted to breaking into things I shouldn't. There are rumors flying around about some of the things I've done. Some are true, a few aren't, but I didn't start any of them. The Bastards know most of my deeds, and while I'd trust them with my life, they know better than to ask for the details of my hacks.

She's not looking at the images I've called up; she's twisted around in the chair, watching me, her eyes intense behind her glasses. "This is a big deal, isn't?"

I go still. I want to deflect, to retreat back into the easy joke, but I force myself to stay right here. "Yeah. I don't share this stuff with just anyone."

No one. That's who's seen what I'm about to show Doc. I tell the Bastards interesting stuff I come across, things that can help us get ahead, but I never let them into my workstation.

My gut twists, my heart gunning like a motor. Do I really trust her this much?

But then I remember the pain in her voice when she told me about her brother. I have to give her this.

"I was poking around the Oakland PD servers," I say, "when I found these files. There wasn't anything else with them—I think someone forgot to erase them from some files they weren't supposed to have."

She puts her chin in her hand as she peers at the screen. Some of her hair falls over her shoulder, revealing a sliver of her neck. "None of these were evidence in the trial. So what cameras are these, and why were the police tracking my brother before they arrested him?"

"Why they were tracking your brother, I can't say. I went through all the data I got off that server but didn't find any other pictures like this."

More of her hair falls forward as she shakes her head, revealing more of her neck. The scent of her skin mixes with her shampoo and tangles in my senses. "It just doesn't compute. Why Ray? He never hurt anyone. Not even when he was having his worst breaks with reality."

"Corvus probably owns the cameras," I say. "I'm guessing they were doing some kind of trial run for the panopticon, something they had to keep secret, but these pictures got left behind when they wiped everything."

She leans back, her head just barely missing my chin. If she takes another half inch, she'll be nestled against me. Her nose flares as she takes a deep breath, then another. A wash of pink comes into her cheeks on the second inhale.

I don't hide my grin when I realize what she's doing—she's *smelling* me. I don't wear cologne or aftershave—the beard means I don't have to shave—so she's smelling just me. And she likes it.

I'd be happy to get that scent all over her later.

She blinks once, long and slow, trying to refocus. "We can't prove that though. And you can't get into Corvus's servers, so we can't see what they have." Her fingers drum on the desk. "These pictures can't help Ray. But something inside Corvus might." She braces her palms against the desk edge as she spins the chair to face me. I have to straighten up and move back to give her room.

I guess we're done with the desk cuddling then.

"Are you sure you can't hack into Corvus?" she asks. The wild hope in her eyes is sharp enough to slice my fingers on.

A spark flies through my brain, gathering energy as it bounces through my skull. There might actually be a way…

"No," I say slowly. "I haven't been able to break into Corvus, not from here."

She slumps in the chair, defeat settling over her. "I thought maybe this time… Maybe this was finally it."

The rest of my plan comes together, my brain slapping the last few pieces into place. It's a little dangerous but not too bad. It's certainly doable.

I've been trying to come up with a plan to crack Corvus for forever. But the variable that had been missing this entire time?

Her.

"I need your help to get into Corvus."

She straightens up in shock and surprise. "I'm not a hacker, not like you." Her mouth drops open as she realizes. "You mean like *physically* getting into Corvus?"

Corvus occupies a SCIF in downtown San Jose—basically a black box of a building. No signal goes in, no signal comes out. And their physical security is as tight as their digital security.

Except I think I know where I can slip in. Where they're not looking too closely.

"I can't get into Corvus myself," I say. At least not as Finn Braden. They'd definitely notice that. "But you… I think you could get in."

We've actually been in the building before together, back when we—all the Bastards and Ultra together—were trying to spring January from Fuchs's clutches.

"They know who I am too." She points to her breastbone. "Remember?"

"Yeah, I remember." She didn't even look twice at me then. Understandable under the circumstances, but I'd still wanted her attention. "I've got a plan for that."

"A plan? A plan to get me inside one of the most secure facilities in the US and then do what?" Her eyebrows nearly hit her hairline. "And then I plant something, install some code somewhere?" She snorts, all ladylike. "It'll never work."

"You won't plant anything. There's no way they'd let you near a computer in that place, at least not an important one."

Relief crosses her face. "So you accept that it's impossible?"

"Nope." Actually, my plan is looking more and more doable. "I can get you inside. Once you're in, I just need you to break something."

My plan is so damn simple it's breathtaking. Corvus isn't going to be expecting simple.

"Break something?"

"Yeah. I need you to break a toilet."

CHAPTER 11

"A toilet?"

I feel like I do when he makes some erratic move in Go that makes no sense whatsoever and could be brilliant or tragic.

Toilets are definitely tragic.

He nods, his mouth set. He looks… determined. Rock steady. When he's wearing that expression, he might be able to convince me of anything.

Capital *T* trouble, like I said.

I blow out a breath. "I have no idea how my breaking a toilet will get you into the back end of Corvus."

He doesn't even blink. I should not find this much self-assurance over breaking a toilet so sexy.

I lift my palms. "How would I even break a toilet?"

Now it's his turn to be skeptical. "You don't know how?"

"No, surprisingly, it's never come up in my life before. I try to keep toilets working as a general rule."

My sarcasm, which was more caustic than hydrochloric acid, only makes him shrug. "Okay, we'll go over some toilet-breaking strategies before I get you inside."

"You're assuming that I'm going to say yes." I lift one eyebrow in challenge.

He crosses those massive arms of his over his massive chest. "You want to stop the panopticon. You want to free your brother. You're going to say yes."

I groan and bury my face in my hands. There's no way he can even get me inside. This entire thing is doomed.

But he's right. I want to do all those things, so of course I'll say yes.

"Has anyone ever told you you're infuriating?" I say through my hands.

"Yeah. You. All the time." The affection in his voice is something new. Warm, comforting. He's not sparring with me, not really.

I let my hands fall away. "Let me say it again then. You're infuriating." There's that same affection, somehow in my voice now. "And there's no way you're getting me inside Corvus."

He winks at me, and my knees go weak. "Leave that part to me. You just worry about breaking the toilet."

"Are you even going to explain the rest of the plan to me?"

"Nope. It'll be a surprise."

"Can you at least tell me how you'll get me into Corvus?"

"Sure. Extreme Doc makeover."

I grab the ends of my hair, remembering all the girls on *America's Next Top Model* sobbing as their hair was chopped into the worst styles. "No. No haircuts, no dyes, no contacts."

He touches my hair, lightly, with one finger. Kind of awed. "I'd never change your hair. It's amazing. You manage to make a totally unnatural color completely you."

I twirl the ends through my fingers. "Thanks. It takes a lot of upkeep, but I love it so much it's worth it."

He keeps stroking my hair, very gently. "The girls in high school wanted hair like this, but they used Kool-Aid to dye it. The color never came out like this."

My body is... *shimmering*. There's no other way to describe the sensation glowing in me. He's so big, just lashed with muscle, so when he's being tender like this, it's head spinning.

"Where are you from?" I ask. In all the profiles I've read of him—not that I've read a ton—it only mentions that he's from "a small town," nothing more specific.

He gives me a considering look, pulling his hand back. "Do you have any idea how I grew up?"

I give a half shrug. "Some suburb of LA? A bedroom community in San Bernardino?" Those places produce a surprising amount of dirt-bike-riding rednecks.

He snorts. "Hell, no. I grew up in a shit hole of a small town where two-thirds of the people were below the poverty line. Not some middle-class suburb with lawns and shit."

That last is aimed directly at me and gets my back up. "And you just assume I'm middle-class?"

He gives me a long, lingering glance, running from my head to my toes. "Look at how you dress," he says. "That's working class?"

I curl my hands into fists. The way I dress says nothing about my background, and I don't have to prove anything to him. "Look at your entire life," I say. "And you're trying to tell me that *you're* working class?"

He opens his mouth to argue some more, then shuts it. A small smile tweaks the corner of his mouth. "Are we really arguing about who grew up poor?"

"Sorry." I drop my gaze. "I get wound up about that stuff. I mean, yeah, I'm making a fair amount of money, but it's all going to Ray's legal bills. My parents cleaned out their savings account, small as it was. They're never going to be able to retire, and I can't help them, not with everything Ray's dealing with."

It's so stupid, because when I see my paycheck, it's an amount that always makes my eyes pop, even after all this time. But then it gets nibbled away so fast.

His expression softens. "Yeah, my parents were in the

same boat. Or at least they were. I grew up in Rancho Carne. It's three hours away from everything."

I blink at him. "But I know where that is. The prison is right there."

"Your brother's there?" Finn shakes his head. "That's crazy. That's only forty-five minutes away."

I know exactly how he grew up now. He wasn't kidding about it being dirt-poor. When I've driven through, there's been nothing but battered trailers, makeshift fences, and scrawny dogs, when there's anything at all. The joke is that the only steady work there is cooking meth. And the town was recently featured in a story on places that didn't have access to clean water. They have to haul in water for everything they need.

"Yeah," he says at my expression. "Exactly that. Don't get me wrong, I had a good childhood. I was loved. I always had enough to eat. But that place… it's like a black hole. You can't escape."

"I grew up in Lancaster."

He gives a low whistle. "So you know what I'm talking about then."

Kind of. Lancaster isn't as bad as Rancho Carne, but it's still the kind of place that's hard to escape. I did, and I thought Ray had, except something much worse was lurking in his own brain.

"How did you get out?" I ask.

Escape wasn't easy for me. I practically gave myself a nervous breakdown in high school, attending classes there and at the local community college, all in an effort to make my transcript as impressive as possible. It worked—I managed to get a full ride to a UC. Not an easy thing to do.

He shrugs as if it was no big deal. "I was always smart and always getting into stuff, pulling it apart to see how it worked, putting it back together with some enhancements. Caltech thought I'd be a good fit."

As if Caltech takes any old student in off the street. No, he had to have done something really impressive to get their attention.

"It's more than that," I say. "Did you win the state science fair or something?"

He shifts as if he's uncomfortable. Like he doesn't want to answer. "Something like that. I won the Westinghouse Science Talent Search."

That's a little bit more than a science fair—that's like winning the science fair for the entire country. And he did it with what must have been minimal resources. A lot of the kids who win that contest have access to full-on research labs.

"Wow," I say.

He shrugs. "It's not such a big deal."

Actually, it is, and I don't know why he's downplaying it. Finn is not the shy type, not by a mile. I decided to let it go. For now. "And now you're a venture capitalist."

He perks up—this is something he's happy to talk about. "Crazy, isn't it?"

His grin is so appealing I have to smile back. "Venture capitalist, hacker, and rescuer of women in your spare time. You're a real Renaissance man."

His gaze darkens. "Please don't do anything like that again. My heart can't take it."

At the mention of his heart, my own starts beating erratically. I can't look away from the swell of his lower lip, half-hidden by his beard, or the dark spark deep in his eyes or the way his big hand rests on the swell of his biceps.

I'm frozen with anticipation. Frozen and on fire, my skin tingling with heat.

"Ramona." He makes my name a gravelly caress. His hand slips into my hair, cups the back of my head, tilts my face toward his. I'm so tight with need the entire sequence is agony, a wait that's so long I'll die.

And then his lips meet mine. His beard isn't at all scratchy but is instead remarkably soft. His skin smells faintly of citrus and sandalwood, the last whisper of his soap from his most recent shower. But the rest is all him.

This kiss is different than our first one. His lips move on mine, his tongue tracing my mouth, all the same movements, but the emotion is very different. That kiss was desperate, but this one is… *recognition.*

I know you, this kiss says. *You know me.*

Our tongues meet, and my pulse explodes. He pulls me up and out of the chair, setting me on the desk. The desktop is hard and cold against my ass. He pushes one thigh, then the other between my legs, the muscles taut and warm.

I want to rub all over him, grind against him until I come with a scream. I want something deeper. Darker. Harder.

He runs his teeth along my throat until I'm panting. My nipples are rock hard, jutting tight against my bra.

His big hand finds my waist, tugging me forward so that we're pressed against each other. I whimper when his chest touches my nipples, lightning forking through me to spear my pussy. I clench around nothing, my body calling out for him.

He tugs at my hair, forcing my head back. My neck is long and exposed, every nerve end sparking, demanding. He holds me there for two heartbeats until he's looked his fill.

When his mouth lowers to my skin, I want to die from sheer relief. And then he uses his lips, his tongue, even his teeth, to savor every inch of my throat, and I really want to die. My neck has always been incredibly sensitive, but he's making every cell in it *sing.*

The rest of my body is taking up the chorus, my breasts, nipples, pussy all humming in time, demanding their turn in the spotlight.

I twist beneath him, needing that relief. My breasts drag

against his chest, and I almost, almost catch my clit on his thigh.

His mouth on my neck is insistent, intense. He's going to leave a mark, and the thought makes me shiver down to my toes. I'll be at work on Monday, wearing a turtleneck, wearing his kisses, and no one will have any clue.

"Ramona," he murmurs against my neck. I twist again, rubbing against him. He lifts his head, but keeps his fingers anchored in my hair. "We can't."

My heart drops to somewhere around my knees. He's right—I definitely don't need this complication.

But God, do I *want* it. I haven't wanted anything just for myself in so long.

I wriggle backward, at least as far as I can with him still holding the back of my head. My body tightens in protest, wanting to be pressed against him again. "Sorry. I lost my head. I should've known better."

He frowns. "Wait, what? I meant I don't have a condom on me. You think this is a mistake?"

"You don't have a condom," I repeat slowly. He just means that we can't fuck on this desk... which leaves open so many more possibilities.

"Sorry, I'm not always prepared," he says, his voice rough. "Never was a Boy Scout."

No, he's definitely no Boy Scout. My heart drums out a hopeful beat. "Um, should we stop completely then?"

His hand tightens in my hair. "No. I owe you an orgasm. And if I don't hear you scream when you come, I'm pretty sure my brain is going to explode." His grin is so wicked it sets my cheeks aflame. "Lady's treat tonight."

"But..." I can't get enough air to speak. "But you could..."

He shakes his head. "I'm greedy. I want to come inside you. Not in your hand, not in your mouth, but in that sweet, wet pussy. And I'm willing to wait for it because I know how good it's going to be."

Fuuuck. I've never in my life had a man speak to me like that. Usually it's *Oh, you feel so good* while they're pumping away, maybe a line or two they've heard in a porno.

But nothing spoken so confidently, so coolly, when we're both fully clothed.

"Oh" is all I can say. I'm witty, I'm smart, I've always got a comeback, but Finn's rendered me speechless.

What a fucking talent.

His smile is so knowing, so triumphant I'd roll my eyes at him any other time. He releases my hair to reach behind me. With one swipe of his arm, he clears the desk—pencils, note-books, and even a tablet falling to the ground in a glorious clatter.

With one finger he pushes me back onto the desk, my legs hanging over the side. "Open your legs." There isn't the slightest trace of amusement there—he's dead serious.

I slip off my shoes, letting them fall to join the rest of the clutter on the floor. Then I set both my heels on the edge of the desk, my thighs open to him.

He crosses his arms, the stern taskmaster demanding more. I've never been into the he-man alpha stuff in the bedroom, but then I've never met a man like Finn before. He challenges me on every level, and I love it.

"Hike up your skirt."

I dig my heels in and lift my hips. I have to wriggle a bit, so I take my time, put on a show. With each inch I reveal, his breath hitches. When I reach the edge of my panties, his hand curls into a fist.

When I pull my skirt all the way up, he moves. Before I can lower my hips, he's got my panties in his fist, pulling them down to my knees. He stops there, swallowing hard. With one finger, he strokes my folds, like he just can't help himself, can't hold back for even a second more. Then he's pulling my panties all the way off, letting them fall from his hand.

The look he's giving me... it steals my breath and thoughts, that kind of hunger. My hips lift involuntary, instinctively reacting to his expression.

He releases a growl, sharp and electric, and then he's pulling my legs open, kneeling between my offered thighs. There's no gentleness, no comfort, and I don't want any. I want it fast and hard and big—as big as he is.

From the first touch, his mouth is devouring, his tongue heavy on my folds. He slides his hands under my ass, lifts me so he can better reach my pussy, so he can shove his tongue so deep inside me my eyes roll back.

I let my hands fall over my head, hanging off the edge of the desk into nothingness. My heels are braced hard against the desk edge because if I let go, I'm going to fall into the vortex of pleasure he's creating with his mouth.

I pull my hand in, find my nipple through my shirt and bra, then squeeze. I bite back a moan as achy need stitches through me from my scalp to my toes.

"So fucking good," he grunts into my pussy, his beard scratching my inner thighs. I'm going to have beard burn between my legs and on my neck, and who knows where else before this is done.

I'm going to masturbate so hard later when I think about those marks.

He finds my clit, doing to it what he'd done to my neck earlier—lighting every nerve end up with his mouth and teeth. I pinch my nipple, sharpening the crest of my oncoming orgasm. I'm so close...

When he slides a finger inside me, first one, then two, then crooks them, I'm done. I grab his head, grinding against his face as I scream and scream, my climax splitting me in two. Or three, or four, or a thousand glittering pieces.

My legs collapse, shaking as my feet dangle off the edge. All of me is shaking, my muscles vibrating with the aftershock of that orgasm. Holy hell.

I close my eyes and simply breathe for long moments. He's still licking me, but it's slow, leisurely, like he can't resist getting one last taste. Then another. And another.

When he raises his head, I gasp. His lips and cheeks and beard are coated with my juices. There's satisfaction in his gaze, hot and sharp. And need, which he's holding back, like a lion on a chain.

He lifts his arm, wipes his face on his sleeve. It's crude and carnal and makes my hips lift, slow as moving through syrup.

He puts a hand on my knee and rubs slow circles with his thumb. I can already feel the burns on my thighs, patches of heat in the cool air running over my naked skin.

"Next time," he says, his voice coming from somewhere deeper than his chest, "I'm not going to forget the condom."

I shiver because this time was mind-blowing. Which means next time…

CHAPTER 12

The high of bringing Doc to a screaming orgasm still hasn't worn off when I walk into my office at Bastard Capital Monday morning.

I sent her home with my driver after that, all bleary and lust dazed. I could have driven her myself, but I was already dangerously close to forgetting I didn't have a condom. I could have stopped at a store, grabbed some, then fucked her all night, but I held back. Being patient always pays off for me, and I knew it would in this instance too.

So I put her in the car, told her we'd talk on Monday about the plan, then sent her off. And then I raced home myself to have a nice, long jerk-off session while I spun dirty fantasies about her and thought more about how we were going to pull off the Corvus heist.

Most of my brainpower went to the fantasies.

I'm at work now, and I've got to look innocent. Or at least like I'm not thinking about her. Normally I wouldn't mind telling the guys about my latest partner—hell, I usually bring it up first—but this thing with Doc feels different. It feels like one of my hacks, as crazy as that sounds. I'll tell them the broad outlines, but the details—I'm gonna be real fucking possessive of the details.

Anjie comes swishing into my office right on cue. "You rang?"

She's wearing a silk dress with parrots on it, a fluffy pink cardigan, and platform heels that add at least six inches to her height. As usual, her makeup is heavy and flawless, and her hair doesn't have a single strand out of place. She looks like she walked in from a picture straight out of the forties, only even glossier.

"Morning," I say. "You have a good weekend?"

She cocks her head. "It was all right. I saw an art show that was awful, then went to a concert that was better. You?"

She raises one eyebrow like she *knows*. Hell, maybe Doc's already told her everything. Which is fine, it's just... I feel like a teenager getting caught necking here.

"Great." I clear my throat, try to be professional, which is tough since it's not something I do often. "I've got a program I need to pass on to one of the start-up teams. One of the ones doing customer behavior—we have any of those?"

Her eyebrow drops. I'm probably just imagining her disappointment. "I think we do. What kind of customer behavior?"

I shrug. Does it really matter? "The algorithm could be modified to do whatever they want, but most companies want to know what triggers people to buy. Isn't that what we're all in search of?"

Anjie points to me. "*You're* not selling anything."

I sold Doc on an amazing orgasm two nights ago, so I'd say I'm a pretty damn good salesman. And that was just the opening bid.

"Well, somebody else always needs to sell something. I'll load it on the server under the usual folder and you can pass it off to one of the start-ups. Then we can start making some money on it."

I pause, remembering Doc's AI, the one she wouldn't let me look at. If I sold that for her, the money would probably help her out a lot. Hell, I could just write a big fat check and wipe out her legal debt with a swipe of my pen—my bank account probably wouldn't even notice—but I don't think she'd like that. She doesn't want to owe me.

Anjie nods as she takes notes on her tablet. "Will do." She fixes me with a look. "How was the press conference Friday?"

I narrow my eyes at her. Does she know what happened? There's something too crafty about her voice. I'm pretty sure I'm not imagining it.

Her eyes are wide and innocent. That Anjie is a sly one, prone to manipulating us in ways we can't even see until it's too late. We don't mind, because she always manipulates us into something good, but I'm wondering if she knew Doc would be at the protest. If Anjie planned for what happened.

No, that's insane. Not even Anjie could have manipulated that situation.

"It was fine," I say. "I was on one side of the barricades listening to the police chief talk about their amazing new crime prediction software and Doc was on the other side with the protesters, shouting that it was all bullshit."

"Oh," Anjie says. "Yep, that sounds like her."

I hadn't known Doc would do something like that until Friday night, and it makes me grumpy that Anjie knew and I didn't. "Anyway, everything was hunky-dory until some asshole threw something at the cops and they went berserk." I clench my jaw, then force my face to relax. "Oh, and Doc fell down in the middle of that fucking mess and almost got trampled to death."

The scene flashes through my mind, my heart racing as if it's happening again.

Anjie gasps, her hand going to her throat. "Oh my God, is she okay?"

"Yeah. I caught her before she went all the way down." Barely. If I'd been just a second too late…

Anjie cocks her head. "You were on the other side of the

barricades, but you managed to spot Doc among the protesters? *And* you caught her before she could fall?"

"What can I say? Superman's got nothing on me."

"Well, she's very lucky you were there. Was she hurt at all?"

Her hands were mostly healed on Saturday—I could tell by the way she moved them, how she pinched hard at her nipple.

"Um, not really." I mentally shake my head, clear my thoughts. "I took her home with me, patched her up."

Anjie purses her lips. "Hmm. That was very nice of you."

"Did you tell Doc that I play Go?"

I don't mean to make that as accusatory as it comes out, but I suddenly can't help it. What has Anjie been up to here?

She taps one manicured finger against her apple-red lips. "I might've mentioned it to her. I can't really remember. We talk about so much stuff. Why? Is there a problem?"

Oh, that's way too casual to be real. Anjie's slipping. I'm not worried that she's gossiping about us outside the office—Anjie would never do that—and I'm guessing that Doc would be too proud to ask about me… but I still came up.

"No," I say. "Doc mentioned it on Friday, and I was just curious about it." I'm as casual as Anjie is. I don't mention that Doc has been setting her AI on me and stalking me through the Go forums. I realize now that was foreplay, and I don't kiss and tell.

"It *is* interesting," she says. "You both play Go and you saved her at the protest…"

I don't finish that for her even though she's dangling it like bait. I don't want Anjie to think she's won. I mean, I love her to death, but a man has to have standards.

"Yep" is all I say.

Anjie raises an eyebrow and lets the moment sit between us. It's the silent treatment, and it's so predictable, but it's still effective. Anjie knows us all better than anyone, so she can pack a lot into her silences.

Finally her mouth curves slightly. "Hmm. So I guess I shouldn't have mentioned you to Doc then. You being *so* uninterested in her."

She spins on her heel, heads for the door. It's a fabulous exit.

"Wait."

Anjie spins back.

I clear my throat. "If Doc ever talks about selling any of her stuff—algorithms, AI—I want to hear about it first. Whatever it costs, we're buying it."

Anjie nods, her expression neutral. "I can do that. Anything else?"

"Um, thanks." I cross my arms. "For telling Doc I play Go."

I'm uncomfortable with even this much rawness—the kind of raw I do isn't emotional—but I really am grateful to Anjie. I want her to know that.

Her smile is warm, like the sun breaking through the clouds. And not at all gloating. "You're welcome. And I'll get that algorithm to one of the start-ups."

Once she's gone, I take a deep breath, rotate my shoulders. Once I'm back to my usual self, I go find Paul. I need to talk to him before the partners' meeting.

He's sitting in his office, talking on the phone in Mandarin. No doubt connecting with one of the many rich and powerful people he knows. Paul comes from old Taipei money, the kind of guy who's the very definition of cosmopolitan: speaks ten languages, thinks nothing about living in London or Singapore or Paris for months at a time.

He also knows everyone. I mean *everyone*. Need a financial whiz who understands cattle futures in Moscow? Paul knows a guy.

I need something simpler though.

I knock quietly at the door in greeting. He nods, his

conversation never slowing. I take a seat in one of the club chairs in his office. Damn, but he's got some nice chairs. They're probably family heirlooms or something, a gift from the last king of Siam. His house is filled with that kind of stuff.

He hangs up and sighs, rubbing between his eyebrows. "Why does immigration have to be such a nightmare?"

"Who were you on the phone with?"

His assistant comes in then, carrying steaming mugs of tea. Paul's not a coffee guy, and I can kind of understand after drinking that tea. It's probably picked by virgins under a full moon or something. Tyler hands me a cup on his way to Paul's desk.

"Thank you," Paul says as Tyler sets a cup in front of him. "Someone I know at the State Department who knows someone at Homeland Security. I'm trying to keep Grace in the country."

Grace was January's roommate; she used to work at Corvus and was here on an H-1B visa. Which meant as long as she had a job at Corvus, she could stay in the country and someday get a green card. Corvus kind of, sort of kidnapped her, entirely legally though. January helped her get out, but now she doesn't have a job and she's got a massive immigration headache instead.

"You're helping and not Elliot?" Elliot is our lawyer and the logical choice for untangling legal issues.

"He is, along with the army of immigration lawyers he's hired just for this. But we thought some… back-channel efforts would help too." He sighs. "Except Arne Fuchs has decided Grace has to be punished for what she did. So he's blocking us at every turn."

"I'm sure you guys will come up with something. It's not like Corvus can buy the entire immigration department."

Paul gives me a skeptical look. "Corvus is doing work for the NSA and the CIA. You really think manipulating immigration and customs enforcement would be difficult for them? They more than know people at Homeland Security; they've got billion-dollar contracts with them."

I don't think I've ever heard Paul sound so defeated. Usually everything is golden with him, even when everything's going to shit.

This is a side of Paul we usually don't see. He's almost always suave, charming, yet aloof. The perfect prince, ideally suited to the wealth and privilege he was born to.

"You okay?" I ask.

There's a flash of annoyance, which he quickly smothers. "Of course. It will all be dealt with in time."

"I've got something you can help me with. Something easy."

He takes a sip of his tea. "Easy sounds good."

"I need an in with a building-maintenance company."

Paul doesn't even blink. He's used to my crazy questions. "Sure. Where and what size? And do I want to know why you want to know?"

"This is definitely need to know."

"Is this a prank or a hack?"

I grin. "It's both. Specifically, I need a maintenance company that deals with SCIFs."

Paul snorts. "You don't ask for much, do you? A SCIF? If this is what I think it is…"

I scoff at the warning in his tone. "Everything will be fine. I'm getting Doc to help me here."

"Oh." Paul leans back in his chair. "I see. You like her."

I roll my eyes. "What the fuck is this, a reality show? Are you all doing confessionals, talking about how you always knew we were perfect for each other?"

Paul smells blood and he loves it. "You know, for a genius, you're pretty fucking stupid. She's not impressed by you, so of course you have to try to impress her. You're smitten."

"*Smitten.* What a dumb word." I'm not smitten, and she's

totally impressed—after an orgasm like that, who wouldn't be?

We're in good old-fashioned lust, nothing more.

Paul just smiles knowingly. Goddamn but he can put a lot of smugness into his expression. "Mark and January are together, Logan and Callie have reconciled, which means you're next. There're just wedding bells everywhere." He makes a motion like he's ringing a tiny bell.

"Why me and not you?"

"If I can dodge my mother's matchmaking attempts, I can dodge fate itself."

"You'd better watch out," I say. "Fate can be a real bitch."

He just keeps looking smug. "I'm not worried about fate. And I'll find what you need. It might take a little bit of time, but it'll happen."

Meaning Paul will pull on all the spiderwebs he's part of, and eventually what I need will fall into his lap.

I wonder if he's ever been disappointed in his entire life. Probably not. I had to earn my confidence, but his is bone deep, implanted there before he was even born.

"Thanks, man," I say. "I owe you."

He turns back to his computer screen. "If you can figure out how to hack into INS and magically fix Grace's visa shit, we'll be even."

"Yeah, Fuchs might notice and raise a stink." I head for the door. "Sadly, not everything can be fixed by fucking around with a computer."

CHAPTER 13

Is this a date?

No, it's not a date.

I can't stop fiddling with my water glass as I wait for Finn. He's chosen a tiny, dark bar in the Fillmore to meet at, and I got here first. It's a bar, so that's a point in favor of a date. But it's also small and decidedly unglamorous—the only other people in here have a couple of decades on us. This is not techbro territory. Points against a date then.

There's an honest-to-God jazz trio playing on the small stage though. And the tables are made for intimacy, for bent heads and whispered conversations.

More points for a date then.

What happened on Saturday in the secure facility confuses everything. Clearly he enjoys my company, he's deeply attracted to me... but he also needs me for whatever he's planning with Corvus.

I never wanted complicated, but I've most definitely got it now.

The Fillmore is known for its music scene, particularly the jazz clubs here. It's a historically black neighborhood, but what with the tech boom and gentrification, there doesn't seem to be much space in the city for anyone who isn't a young white male working in tech. But the Fillmore still has enough of its old character left to make it unique.

When Finn walks in, every head in the café turns toward him. But of course they would—he's well over six feet, wearing enough muscle to pass as a power lifter, and his beard… I can't describe his beard as anything but primal.

A shiver runs over my skin as I remember how his beard felt on my thighs, coarse yet gentle, a subtle contrast to the soft urgency of his lips. I've still got a hint of redness on my inner thighs, which I've been surreptitiously running my fingers over all day.

I can tell from the way some of the women in the café are watching him that they're imagining some of the same things involving his beard. I'm half tempted to stand up on a chair and announce *What you're all imagining? I actually got to do*!

But that would be bragging. In life, as in Go, you should accept your victories humbly.

Finn folds himself into the chair across from me. "What's got you looking like that?"

"Like what? I don't look like anything." I was practicing being humble, which he probably doesn't recognize since he never practices it himself.

"Like you know something that everyone else here doesn't."

So much for looking humble. Before I can come up with an excuse for my expression, he flags down a passing waiter.

"Jack and Coke," he says, an easy command.

I'm surprised by that. As far as cocktails go, it's not a particularly inventive one, and Jack Daniel's isn't exactly a well-respected whiskey.

"You know, they have better stuff than that."

"I know." He sets one heavy elbow on the table, closing us into a more intimate space. "But sometimes I just want a Jack and Coke. I drank a lot of those in college, and it's like taking a walk down memory lane."

It's odd; he's got more money than any rational person would know what to do with, but he's also very… earthy. Take the dirt bikes—most men in Silicon Valley like fast, luxurious cars. Things they can show off on private race-courses to their equally wealthy friends. Not something you take out to a dirty, dusty desert trail, blasting around with your high school friends.

"You only want water?" he asks when the waiter comes back.

"I wasn't sure…" I bite my lip.

"Wasn't sure what?"

I glance at the waiter, then back at Finn. "I wasn't sure if this was a date."

The waiter keeps his face very professionally neutral.

"I'm not into labels," Finn says. "It's whatever you want it to be."

His eyes darken though, making me think of that desk and his head between my thighs. He was going to make sure he had condoms next time…

"I'll have a gin and tonic," I say, my skin tingling. "Lots of ice."

I'll need it if I'm ever going to cool down after this.

"So," I say once the waiter's gone again, "do you come here often? I like it, but I wouldn't have said it was your style."

"Once in a while." He shrugs. "You have to be the right kind of person to appreciate this place."

"And you think I'm the right kind of person?"

He looks me up and down, taking in my purple hair, my thick, fashionable glasses, and my button-down shirt embroidered with tiny grinning skulls. "Was I wrong?"

I look around the bar, which is packed with more atmosphere than ought to fit. I could sit here for hours with him, sipping my drink and just soaking him up.

"No," I say. "This place is awesome." I give the waiter a

grateful smile when he brings my drink, which is brimming with ice.

I take a long, delicious, refreshing sip. There's nothing like a gin and tonic after a long day at work, and they didn't skimp on the gin.

When I sigh, Finn goes stiff.

"What's wrong?" I set down my glass, leaning in toward him.

"When you sigh…," he mutters under his breath.

Oh, this is interesting. I rest my cheek on my hand, getting even closer. "When I sigh what?"

He comes so close our noses are almost touching, and we can only breathe the other's exhales. "When you sigh, it makes me so fucking hard."

The entire bar has stopped—they must have stopped—because even though he said it only for me, everyone had to have felt the shock wave from that.

"My sigh?" I don't understand; it's an ordinary sigh.

"Yeah. It's like you're sliding into the warmest bath, eating the richest chocolate…" His voice drops even lower. "Having the best orgasm."

I search for a snappy retort, but all that comes to mind is *Holy hell.* Not at all snappy.

"Wow" is what I say.

"Exactly." He leans back, takes a drink, and I feel like I can breathe again.

I take a long sip of my own drink. Alcohol isn't exactly head clearing, but it's better than hearing that my sighs make him hard. And I really, really want to know more about this plan of his.

"Are you going to explain about the toilet now?"

He flashes a smile. "The toilet is the easy part. Don't you want to hear about how I'm going to get you into Corvus?"

"Sure." I lean back, raise my eyebrows. "It should be an

interesting plan since getting into Corvus will be impossible. I've been there before—they've got my picture on file."

"We'll do a makeover. You won't look like yourself."

I can't believe he's saying that like he really believes it. "First off, facial-recognition software doesn't care if you've had a makeover." I point to my hair. "And if you think I'm going to alter this after what I paid for it—"

"I already told you I love your hair." He's offended I would even suggest it. "I've written enough facial-recognition software to know what it is and isn't capable of."

"Wait…" Realization slowly dawns on me. "What facial-recognition software *have* you written?"

Bastard Capital invested in a very famous start-up a few years back, a company that sold its facial-recognition system to the biggest social media site for hundreds of millions. I have a sudden suspicion Finn actually wrote it.

"Do I really need to tell you?" he asks. "Come on, you're smart."

I am, but not like he is. Jesus, how many more start-ups have come out of Bastard Capital selling his ideas? And he's never put his name to one of them. I don't get it.

I toss back the rest of my drink, needing a moment. "A makeover. Okay. As long as my hair isn't touched." I swirl the ice left behind. "And what exactly am I supposed to be doing at Corvus? I can't just walk in and announce I'm there for their toilets."

He smiles with one side of his mouth, which is way too endearing. "Should I get you another drink?"

I shake my head. The one is enough, especially if I'm going to keep up with him.

"You're going to be interviewing for a job," he says. "They've been looking for someone to work in their native AI division for forever. And nobody knows AI better than you."

Actually, there are a ton of people who do, him included. But I know enough to get myself through a coding interview.

"But they have to actually invite me in for an interview." Has he forgotten that part?

"I've already written up a fake résumé for you with all the right keywords that will trigger their automatic screens. Trust me, they'll be dying to meet you."

"Oh Lord. If you've made me out to be some kind of supergenius, they're going to see right through me." My palms are sweating just thinking about it. I do know a fair amount about AI but to be grilled—and *fail*—in the belly of the beast?

"You *are* a supergenius." He says that so casually I know he really means it. Even though I'm sitting down, my knees go weak. "You'll be fine. In fact, if you weren't a fake, you'd be perfect for the job."

"Oh yeah, I'd only be working for *Corvus* then. Otherwise it'd be perfect." I sip some of the water left in my glass to wet my dry throat. "What happens if they figure out who I really am?"

They practically took Grace prisoner—moving her to company housing, cutting off all her outside access, making her work fourteen-hour days.

"They won't." There's steel in his voice, steel that stiffens my spine. "The backstory I made for you is airtight."

"Backstory?" I have an invented backstory?

"I invented a whole life and career for you and seeded it in the appropriate places online. Turns out you graduated from MIT with honors, worked in a few start-ups along the way, and now you're ready to move on to the big boys." He waves a large hand. "Of course, we both know you're way too smart for MIT, but they don't know that."

I have to smile, because even in the middle of planning a break-in at the most secure building in California, he can't let the Caltech-MIT rivalry go.

"Have you ever done something like this before?" I ask. "Physically going into a place where you're not supposed to instead of just virtually."

"Not exactly this, but yeah, I've done similar stuff to get into places where I want to go."

It's the strangest thing to be turned on by, but I am. *Where I want to go*—if he wants to, he does it. And he doesn't let anything stop him.

He wanted to give me an orgasm, and boy howdy, did he. I wonder how many condoms he's got in his wallet right now.

"Is it true you hacked into the NSA to change all their screen savers to memes?"

He lets out a short laugh and points to my phone, which is sitting on the table. "You might be running Ultra Encryption, but I'm still not going to confess with a recording device right there." His expression shifts, goes hard. "Remember how Mark was when Fuchs tried to take January?"

"Yes. I didn't think he had that in him." Mark's a deal-maker, always suave but looking for an in. When he went to rescue January... It was like a dragon had awakened within.

"Well, remember how Mark was. And imagine how *I'll* be if that happens to you."

I run my gaze over him, from his thick hair, his hard gaze, his wild beard, then those strong shoulders, wide chest, massive arms. I swallow hard when I imagine exactly what he told me to.

Something unknots in my chest. Yes, this will be dangerous and crazy and nerve shattering, but I'm doing it for Ray. If I can spend everything I have on legal fees, I can do this. And if I fall, Finn will be there to catch me.

Which raises the question: "What do you want out of all this? Just to prove you can?"

"You want your brother out. And I've wanted to get into Corvus for forever. We'll both get what we want."

I shift in my seat. It shouldn't matter that Ray isn't his first priority, because why would he be? Finn's never met my brother. Ray's my responsibility.

And even if what we find doesn't free Ray, it might be enough to stop the panopticon. If I can stop someone else from suffering what Ray did, will all this still be worth it?

I frown at myself. Of course it will. If I can demonstrate to the world how wrong the panopticon is, how we have to cling to our ideals of innocent before proven guilty, then yes, it will definitely be worth it.

"What's wrong?" Finn asks.

I smooth out my expression, my resolve cementing into place. I'm going to sneak into Corvus, then help Finn sneak in. There was never any other choice for me.

"Nothing," I say. "First off, I'm going to need another drink. And second, when are we starting this makeover?"

His expression lifts into savage triumph. "Tonight," he says. "Oh, have I got plans for you."

CHAPTER 14

Finn at least let me finish my second gin and tonic after that announcement, although he was practically vibrating with impatience. He's not one for delayed gratification when it comes to his hacking schemes, I guess.

The bedroom seems to be a different story. We've had drinks, we're on our way to Union Square, just us two in his Tesla, but he hasn't said a single word about his plans for me beyond a makeover. And I know he's got them—the hot spark I see in his eyes when I catch him glancing at me proves it.

Well, two can play that game. And we've proven that we're very good at playing games together.

Once the car is parked—delivered to a valet in a parking garage, actually—we walk through Union Square. It's surprisingly quiet, probably because today is cold, the wind blowing in frigid air from the ocean. Saks Fifth Avenue looks out loftily over it all, Tiffany's sitting right next to it. The Sir Francis Drake peeks out over it, just half a block up.

I'm not a usual visitor to Union Square. The stuff I can afford here is more for tourists. And the expensive stuff... Well, let's just say that Tiffany's was never on my shopping list even before I drained my savings.

Finn knows right where he's going, taking my hand and leading me across the square. When we walk into the Ferragamo store, I bite back my protest.

The interior is so sleek it hurts. There're no racks of clothes, trays of accessories, or rows of shoes. Heck, they don't even have a bunch of nooks with handbags sitting in them like the Coach store.

Oh no, this store is way too chic for that. There are a few dresses hanging on dummies, shoes and a handbag at their feet, but it's clear you don't come in here for a casual shopping excursion. Lookie-loos are not welcome.

The clothes themselves scream *Politician's wife*, all inoffensive colors and lines. I am so fucking far from that kind of woman it's not even funny. And Finn thought it would be appropriate to take me into this store? Doesn't he even want me to look human after this makeover?

The salesman comes over to us, a slim, handsome man in his midtwenties, looking model perfect in his well-cut suit. I can see the calculations working behind his eyes. Finn's still wearing his sunglasses, and with his beard and the tattoo peeking out from under his collar, he looks like a biker from a funeral who stumbled into the wrong store.

And me... I glance down at my outfit. I'm definitely into hipster style, which isn't even in the same universe as the clothes in this place.

The salesman blinks once, twice, then smiles. To his credit, only the edges are strained. "What can I help you with today?"

Finn whips off his sunglasses, and recognition steals over the salesperson's features. But he's too well-trained to actually say anything.

"She needs a suit for an interview," Finn says. He looks almost baffled by the store, and I'm tempted to ask him what the hell he was thinking, bringing us here.

"Of course," the salesperson says.

An hour later, I'm dressed like I haven't been since my grad school interviews. The suit is gray, the kind of gray that makes me think of being depressed, and it's cut so severely you could injure yourself on it. Underneath is a lilac camisole, the exact same shade as my hair, not that I think it was intentional. On my feet I've got low-heeled shoes with gold buckles, perfect for pretending I'm a pilgrim at the first Thanksgiving. I look poised, accomplished, and fearless. I also look nothing like myself from the neck down.

I take a moment to stare myself down in the mirror. This is who I have to be if I'm going to get through this without raising suspicion.

This woman went to MIT, got a cushy job right out of school. She's done everything right, is sailing up the corporate ladder. Someday she'll be in a corner office.

She definitely doesn't have a brother in prison. She wouldn't be caught dead at a protest.

I can feel the character taking shape in my head, can see all the ways she'd respond to things, so very differently from me. As she forms, she reminds me a lot of Minerva Dyne.

I wear this woman's character on my face as I walk out of the dressing room. I raise my hands and do a little twirl for him.

I half expect Finn to applaud, but instead he frowns. Fiercely.

The salesman is instantly distressed. "Is this not what you had in mind?"

Finn continues to frown. "No, it is. It's just…" His eyes meet mine. I smile and shrug, because he wanted me to look different, didn't he? *Be* different? He can't complain when I am.

Finn doesn't smile back. Instead, he tugs at his beard. "Yeah," he says slowly. "That's exactly what I wanted. I just wasn't expecting Ramona to look so different."

He's used my given name before, but it still sends a warm,

tingling shock through me. Almost no one calls me that—I've been Doc since the day I was granted my PhD. Sometimes people will try calling me Ramona at first, but sooner or later, everyone comes around to Doc.

Oh shit. I'm going to have to answer to a fake name the entire time. Jesus, I hope I can remember and not give myself away.

"It's perfect," Finn announces.

I turn around to head back to the dressing room, ready to get this suit off.

"Nope," Finn says, stopping me dead. "Wear it out."

If Finn has handed off his credit card at any point, I don't see it. Instead of dealing with the payment, he hustles me out of the store, instructing the salesman to wrap up my old clothes and send them to him.

The second we're outside, I stop. "Why can't I change? And when do I get my old clothes back?"

He grabs my hand, pulls me forward. "We need to make sure the wig fits with this. And once we're done, I've got a surprise for you."

"A wig?"

He glances at me over his shoulder. "I told you I love your hair and nothing will happen to it."

"What kind of a wig?" I ask. "I'm not wearing some kind of stupid Halloween thing."

He rolls his eyes. "I want this to be convincing. Look at how much we just spent for the suit. You really think I'd buy a cheap wig?"

I raise an eyebrow. "*We* spent on the suit?"

"Well, we're in this together. So yes, *we* spent. Besides, what the hell would I do with a woman's suit?"

I honestly don't know what I'll do with this suit afterward —maybe run for office?—but I drop it.

He leads us into a nondescript high-rise where a doorman guards the entrance.

"Mr. Braden," the doorman says in greeting. "Ms. Dogaru is expecting you."

We take the elevator up a dozen floors, then walk into a hallway with dozens of doors, all of them with discreet nameplates next to them. COLERIDGE AESTHETICS, reads one. DECCA THOMPSON TRAINING reads another.

I'm guessing this is where the richest women in the City come to keep themselves toned and beautiful. I guess wigs would be part of that.

Finn knocks on a door with a nameplate that reads MS. DOGARU, nothing else. Wigs must be a need-to-know kind of business.

An hour later, I'm having the time of my life. Ms. Dogaru turns out to be full of sass, and even though I'm getting a boring brunette bob—think Anna Wintour, only more severe—she's keeping me entertained.

"Here we are," she says, giving the wig one last tweak. "It's not quite boring but not really noticeable either."

When I look at myself in the mirror, I'm startled. If I were to pass my reflection on the street, I wouldn't know myself.

One more bit of this new character snaps into place. It's almost like I'm building a program, except it's a person. As I'm deciding how this person is, how she'd react to things, I'm basically building subroutines my new character will be running as part of her personality.

This time when I come out, Finn doesn't frown. He doesn't smile either, but he definitely looks satisfied.

"Perfect," he says. "Well, not perfect—you looked way hotter before—but perfect for what we need."

I spin around, showing off the entire transformation. "What, you don't like me as president of the garden club? Or the free world?"

"You don't look like the president of the garden club," he says. "You know who you do look like? Minerva."

Without even thinking about it, I gently punch him in the

stomach. "That's a low blow." Although I was thinking that myself in Ferragamo, he could have the decency not to say it.

He just laughs at my feeble attempt to wound him. "But you do. And we know that Fuchs is in love with Minerva, so it works perfectly."

I don't think Fuchs loves anything, much less Minerva, but he certainly keeps her close.

Finn nods to Ms. Dogaru, who disappears into one of the back rooms.

"Is it safe to talk about this in front of her?" I ask.

"Oh yeah. She's got much bigger secrets than this."

I can see that. "So, is this all I need to fool the facial-recognition systems?"

"No, there's one last thing. I've got some glasses for you to wear, ones that I've modified."

Before he can explain more, Ms. Dogaru comes back. I gasp when I see what's in her hands.

The only way to describe it is mermaid hair. It's not bright or garish, and the strands look whisper soft. It's muted blues, soft greens, gentle purples—exactly the kind of hair a mermaid in a story would have.

My fingers flex instinctively. I want that hair. Or wig. Or whatever. I just need it.

"Is that for me?" I almost whisper. I don't usually flip out over stuff, but that wig is so me it hurts.

"No, it's for me," Finn deadpans. "I thought it would look good with my beard."

Ms. Dogaru laughs. I resist the urge to punch him again, because she's pulling off the other wig and setting the mermaid hair on my head.

"Oh." It's all I can say when I see myself in the mirror. This wig is a fantasy, the very best kind. It looks strange with the suit I'm in, but I'm already putting together the perfect outfit for it in my head. Except… this thing has to be expensive. It's too high quality to be anything but.

Finn's mouth flattens when he catches my expression. "It's yours," he says. "This is your surprise. One of them at least."

I touch one of the curls, shot through with soft aqua and highlighted with sea blue. I feel like myself in this wig, only better. More beautiful. More striking. Exactly the opposite of how I felt in the other wig.

"He picked it out himself," Ms. Dogaru says with a significant look.

Finn doesn't flinch or blush or look away from me for a second. "As soon I saw it, I knew."

I blush for both of us even though I'm not usually a blusher. "I guess I'll have to take it then."

There's a knock at the door, breaking the spell between Finn and me.

"There's your clothes," he says.

Sure enough, there's a courier at the door with a package, which turns out to be the clothes I'd left behind at Ferragamo. Ms. Dogaru takes me to a back room where I can change. I'm so relieved to get back into my old clothes, although it hurts to give back the mermaid wig.

"I'll wrap all this up, including the clothes, and send it to your suite," Ms. Dogaru says with a wink.

Suite? I don't know anything about that, but I figure it's better to ask Finn about that than Ms. Dogaru.

Which I do as soon as we're in the hallway.

"What suite?" I ask. My head's already spinning from everything else—what more can he have planned?

"I figured we'd spend the night in the City," he says. As if it's just too much trouble to cross the Bay Bridge.

It does seem very far suddenly, Berkeley and Oakland and the rest of the East Bay. And there are so many hotels right next door… Luxury hotels…

"Sounds good," I say, because I'm not ready for this fantasy to end.

CHAPTER 15

Doc's reaction when we pull up to the Fairmont Hotel, perched high atop Nob Hill with all the flags fluttering over the entrance, is exactly what I'm hoping for.

"Of course you would pick the hotel with a tiki bar," she says.

"Who doesn't want a rainstorm *in the restaurant* while they're eating?" I ask as I help her out of the car.

"I want a mai tai in a glass so big I can swim in it."

"And afterward you'll jump in the lagoon?"

"Maybe. I'm betting I can't get kicked out if I'm with you."

Considering that I've booked the Penthouse Suite on a whim, which costs more nightly than most people's yearly mortgage payment, probably not.

I toss the keys to the valet, then take her hand and lead her into the foyer. "I'd rather not spend tonight fishing you out of a bar pool," I say. "And I've already arranged for mai tais in the room." I lean in toward her ear. "I'm sure it's big enough even for you."

She laughs as we head for the elevators. When I insert my key to call the penthouse elevator, she asks, "You don't even have to check in?"

"You haven't figured out by now that when I do something, I take care of everything?"

The look she gives me sets my blood on fire. "Trust me, I'm getting the point."

The elevator doors ding, then sweep open. I put a hand to the small of her back and guide her in. "Oh, there still a lot more for you to get."

We ride up to the very top floor in silence, but the air practically pulses between us. I've never been this *aware* of a woman before. When she breathes, every inch of my skin comes to attention. When she shifts, my libido snarls and snaps, wanting to be closer to her. To imprint myself on her.

The elevator opens into a postage-stamp-sized hallway that leads to a set of double doors.

"After you." I gesture her forward.

She looks back at me as she heads out, as if she can't bear to look away for even that bare amount of time.

I know the feeling.

When the doors open and she steps in, she gasps. "Oh my God."

The Penthouse Suite is a trip. There's a 360-degree view of San Francisco, a telescope set up so you can better see the Golden Gate, a terrace done in a riot of colors, and a billiard room done in tiles from a Turkish hamam. With every room Doc walks through, her eyes get bigger.

We finish the tour in the two-story library filled with built-in shelves and capped off with a rotunda.

"It's like *Beauty and the Beast*," Doc murmurs. Her gaze runs over me. "Only you've got more hair."

I run my hands through my hair. "Didn't he have horns too?"

"Yep. And fangs." But she looks intrigued rather than appalled.

I can show her my fangs then. But first: "There's a secret passage too. Supposedly Marilyn Monroe snuck through it when she was visiting JFK and Jackie came back to the room."

She makes a face. "That's way less romantic than *Beauty and the Beast.*"

"Real life is usually less romantic than a Disney movie." I move closer to her, cutting the distance between us. "I didn't think you were a romantic. An idealist, yes, but not a romantic."

"It's a gorgeous library. Any woman who doesn't swoon over this must be dead."

"You don't look dead to me." I touch her cheek, brushing it with the tips of my fingers. Her skin is so soft it can't be real. But it is. "Does that mean you're swooning?"

"My pulse *is* racing." Her tongue slips out to wet her lips, and now *my* pulse is racing.

I put my arms at her back and knees and sweep her up. "I'd better catch you before you fall then." I start off for the master bedroom—we can order more mai tais from room service once we're done. Sometime tomorrow morning.

"You're very good at it." Her hand cups my neck, her fingers sliding into my hair. Her touch is light, but my entire body responds.

I don't want to think about her falling in that crowd, about how close I was to not catching her. Instead, I lower my mouth to hers.

She tastes of her gin and tonic, sharp, refreshing, and that sweetness that's unique to Doc underneath it all. Her hand tightens on my neck, pulling our faces closer. Her lips are hungry, demanding—this woman doesn't hold back.

Good, because neither do I.

When we arrive in the master bedroom, I toss her onto the California king, then start tearing off my clothes. She does the same, the two of us in a fury to be naked. I guess it'd be more romantic for me to slowly strip her, but I'm not feeling the least bit romantic. I feel like a goddamn beast.

She pulled off her glasses at some point, is stripping off her bra, then shimmies out of her panties, and I have to stop and catch my breath. She's just… I swallow hard. Her tits are glorious—how the fuck did she hide *those* under her shirts?—her waist has tighter curves than Le Mans, and her ass has even juicer curves than that.

"Fuck," I hiss out. My cock twitches, pulling against my belly.

Doc spreads herself out on the bed, my sexual fantasies made flesh. "Is that a good fuck or a bad fuck?"

I climb over her, lingering over her sweet body. "That's a *holy fuck*. And I'm going to show you an amazing fuck tonight."

With a quick flip that has her gasping, I put her on top. Her breasts sway, so full and heavy I want to cry. Or get on my knees and thank God for making such perfect breasts.

I take two handfuls of her ass and start to knead. Okay, now this really makes me want to cry and sing hallelujah, because this is the sweetest ass I've ever held. Taut but yielding and just the perfect handful.

She sets her hands on my shoulders and slides forward, her pussy rubbing against my happy trail. And she's already *wet*.

My cock jerks, straining hard toward her. We haven't even done anything yet, and my dick is already going nuts. I haven't been this horny ever, not even when I was a teenager and creaming my sheets every night in my sleep.

I'd better give her that *amazing fuck* before my cock embarrasses me here.

I tug her forward, pulling her hips up over my belly, then my chest, and finally over my shoulders so that she's sitting on my face. I inhale deeply—aroused Doc is rapidly becoming my favorite scent in the whole world.

"Finn?" *Really?* her tone asks.

I blow on her curls in answer. She gives a strangled moan, her thighs tightening around my ears. Music, sweet music.

Slowly, deliberately, I lick her pussy with the flat of my tongue. She tastes like the ocean, if it were made of pure desire.

She does that sigh of hers, the one connected straight to my cock. I hold her hips steady, angling her clit just so. I tease it first with my tongue—it's all swollen and slippery. Her hands slide into my hair, curling into fists. The pain is just this side of sweet, lightning traveling from my scalp to storm through my belly and thighs and balls.

I kiss her clit, a little motion to say hello, and she whimpers. Her hips buck, but I force her to keep still. She's not getting away from this.

I close my lips around her clit and suck, gently at first, then not so gently. Her moans go high and loud, her fingers practically tearing at my scalp. I love it, every second of her wildness, so I suck harder.

When she grinds against my face, driving toward her climax, I nearly come myself. She's so greedy, so willing to just grab her pleasure and squeeze it as hard as she can.

I can feel the waves of her orgasm building in the flutter of the muscles under my tongue, the way her taste changes. Soon enough, she's going to ride my cock like she's riding my face. My own climax threatens at the thought, but I force it back. I meant it when I said I was going to come inside her and nowhere else.

Finally her hands relax on my scalp. Then she releases my hair with a start. "Oh shit." She wriggles backward before I can stop her. "I think I tore out some of your hair. Are you okay?"

I have to laugh, because I literally can't feel a thing except the pressure in my cock and balls, demanding release. "That was nothing. Not even a love bite."

Her eyes darken, although she's only just come. Thank

God women don't need to recover after an orgasm. "How many condoms did you bring?"

"I bought out the drugstore."

Her lips curve. "Ambitious, aren't we?"

"You inspire me to new feats of strength."

This time her fingers curl into the hair on my chest. "Show me."

I pull out the drawer in the bedside table, and her eyes go wide. "Holy hell," she says, her eyes wide when she sees all the Trojan Magnum boxes there. "You really did buy out the drugstore."

I grab one and reach around her to put it on. She takes advantage of the opportunity to run her nails along my abs.

"I didn't think bodies like this existed in the real world," she says wistfully.

"I could say the same about yours." With the condom on, I lie back, take her in. I could lose myself in her curves for the rest of my life.

Taking my time, I run my hands over her waist, down her hips, up her rib cage. Her skin is so soft my fingers start to shake, my senses going into overload. She watches me with a hooded gaze, accepting my worship, reveling in it.

Her breasts are incredibly tempting with hard, dark nipples jutting proudly, but I leave them for last. Touching those will have me redlining in seconds.

Instead, I do something I've never done before: I pull myself up so that she's sitting on my lap and we're face-to-face. I can see details I never could before—the freckle under her eye, a tiny scar on her forehead that's usually hidden by her glasses, the divot in her upper lip that kisses the bow of her mouth. My heart does something I can't describe as I take in this closeness, this newness.

She's taking me in too, her gaze softening. That softness compels me to lean in and kiss her. This kiss starts out not soft, exactly, but not devouring like our others have been. This kiss can take its time.

But then it turns to kindling, then to flame, and finally to an inferno. Our hips are rocking together, my cock siding through her hot folds, our mouths fused.

I grab her hips, lift her without breaking the kiss, then lower her onto my cock. Slowly, to give her time to adjust but also to savor the little moans she makes as I do. When I'm balls deep in her—fuck, but she's so perfectly snug, so deliciously hot—she does that sigh. And my cock swells.

She sets her hands on my shoulders and shoves me down, just rough enough. "I want to ride you."

A mind reader. Not only is she wicked sharp, super snarky, and drop-dead gorgeous, she can read my mind in bed. I put my hands behind my head and thrust up, watching every bit of her bounce as I do. "Sure. Do you want a bucking bronco or a sweet little pony?"

When she laughs, her pussy clenches around me. I have to smother a groan.

"How about…?" She raises her arms over her head, pulls that beautiful hair up and lets it fall all over her shoulders. "How about we start with bucking bronco"—she runs a nail down my chest—"then I tame you into a sweet little pony?"

"Mmm." I jerk my hips up, just to let her know what she's dealing with. "If you think you can."

Her smile is a curve of challenge. And when she starts to move, I'm almost lost. I've waited so damn long for this woman—or at least it feels that way—that I'm on edge, ready to release.

I rock into her, finding her rhythm, making sure to put pressure on her clit. Her pulse hammers in her throat, and her breathing goes quick and shallow. Her inner muscles clench, and my balls draw up tight in response.

She fucks me harder, running her hands over her stomach, her ribs, ghosting her palms over her breasts, high-lighting every curve I love.

When she gets to her nipples, I growl, "Pinch them."

First she takes her lower lip between her teeth, like she's readying herself. And then she takes her nipples between her thumbs and forefingers and squeezes.

Her sigh is a long, luxurious ripple, wrapping around the both of us as we pump into each other. And then her sigh goes low, guttural, and transforms into a moan as she comes.

I grab her hips to hold her tight and finish up with one, two hard thrusts, all of me straining to be with her in the climax. I erupt into her, my whole body seizing as I come harder than I have… ever.

Limp and sticky and sweaty, we collapse together in the bed, my arms over hers, her arms tossed over mine, our legs too tangled to know who's who.

I want to say something, to mark this moment, to do something besides hold her and pass out. But maybe that's enough.

Still, I reach for something. I'm a smart fucker, I should be able to come up with something witty.

But instead all I get out is a weak "Pony?"

She snorts with muffled laughter against my shoulder, sounding as tired as I feel. "Bronco," she says, letting me win. "Bronco all the way."

CHAPTER 16

Finn turned out to be a cuddler.

He kept me close all night, even when we weren't fucking like crazy. He wasn't kidding about his stamina or my inspiring him to feats of strength. And when we came down from each and every high, he pulled me close and kept me there.

So when I wake up nestled next to him, I'm not surprised. There hasn't been more than six inches between us since he showed me the library.

I nibble my lip as I watch him sleep. I have to get up, get to work, but he looks so… I frown as I try to pin down how he looks. Not sweet or boyish or tender. He just looks like someone I want to keep looking at.

Aw, hell. I have no idea where we're going after we do this insane break-in, if we're even going anywhere. I should ask him, straight out, but I don't want to. I want to keep assuming this will last, that I will get to keep looking at this person.

I swallow hard. If I squint, I can convince myself that with everything going wrong in my life, I deserve the fantasy. Just for a little bit longer. It's such a beautiful one.

He starts to smile even before he opens his eyes. "Are you watching me?" he asks with his eyes still closed.

"I'm not going to answer that."

His smile gets wider. "You can admit it. I promise not to get a big head. At least not with *that* head."

I know now how big his other head can get. I'm going to be deliciously sore all day from last night. Which brings me back to the sad fact that I have to be at work soon.

"I should get going," I say, sitting up and pulling the sheet around me. I can scrub most of his scent off in the shower—God, I'll miss it—do what I can with the makeup in my purse, and head in to the office in yesterday's clothes. I've got a change of clothes in my desk, so if I get really lucky, no one will know I've been up all night with Finn.

January's not the kind to squee, but if she hears about this, she'll start imagining triple dates with her, Mark, Logan, and Callie, and dreaming of us as best couple friends. I'm not ready to deal with that, not with everything else going on.

Finn shifts so he can wrap himself around me again, his arm coming over my crossed legs. "They're bringing breakfast in a minute. Steak and eggs."

My stomach rumbles. I'm not the kind to skip breakfast—I get cranky if I don't get some food and coffee in me before I start the day. And steak and eggs is a pretty good way to start the day.

"Well…" I don't really *have* to be in by nine on the dot. And if it's already on the way…

He pats my ass. "And we have to talk about what happens next."

My heart dives for my feet. He wants to talk about a relationship? Already? My heart starts climbing, soaring, because this is actually a good thing—and then I catch sight of his expression as he unfolds from the bed.

He means the break-in. Not anything else.

I firmly set my heart back where it belongs. "Right. I've got an interview to prep for."

By the time I'm out of the shower and in yesterday's clothes, breakfast has been set up in the kitchen nook. This room has a kitchen, which probably no one ever uses, that's bigger than my entire apartment.

Finn's waiting for me at the table, in fresh clothes, his hair and beard damp. He must have had them sent over. He's got a laptop open—no morning papers for him—and is scrolling and typing with intense focus.

"Just dealing with Slack," he says without looking up. His plate sits in front of him, untouched.

The moment my bottom hits my chair, he snaps the laptop shut, giving me his full attention.

"Morning, sunshine," he says with a half smile.

"Morning." I dig into my steak, determined to be my usual, snappy self. "Did you sleep well?"

He laughs softly. "Perfectly."

Oh, my heart. It slips out of place before I can catch it. "What do I do next?" I ask, staring at my eggs.

"I'll arrange everything else." His voice is brisk. "You just treat it like any other coding interview."

Okay, I have to give him a look at that. "People spend months prepping for coding interviews. There are entire books—dead-tree books—devoted to the coding interview."

"You'll do fine." He's not even dented by my skepticism.

"I guess I can get January to help me run through some stuff."

"No." His gaze snaps to mine. "Don't tell anyone. Not even January."

A chill runs over me, more nerves than cold fear. "I understand we have to be careful, but my telling January is like your telling the rest of the Bastards."

"Which I haven't done."

I blink at him. "You haven't?"

"No. Once it's finished, I'll give them the highlights, but that's it. They know how I work."

But that's not how I work, with everything secret, closed off. My friends know about my AI, know about my brother, know me.

It hits me then—Finn might seem open, friendly, nothing to hide when you first meet him, but underneath… I might not know what's really underneath.

"I'm beginning to think I don't know you at all," I say slowly.

His expression is slightly wounded. "Of course you do."

Something about the way he's acting reminds me of when he was talking about winning the Westinghouse contest in high school—not exactly ashamed but definitely closed off. Like it meant too much to him to talk about openly.

Like I mean too much to him to talk about openly.

I don't know how to process that or if I'm even right about all this assuming I'm doing about him. So instead, I start to grill him about AI, which is a much safer topic. Soon enough, we're going back and forth, bouncing ideas off each other, picking apart the faults and having a grand time. My mind is humming with things I want to try with the code, things I can't wait to discuss with him once I've tested them.

Too soon, breakfast is over. Finn pushes away from the table and watches me for a long moment. He looks like he's considering something, something I might say no to.

But all he says is "There's a car and driver waiting for you out front." There's a faint thread of regret in his voice.

There's more than a faint thread of regret in me, but work calls.

"Thanks for breakfast," I say, gathering my things. "It was great." I open the front door and walk into the hallway before this gets even more awkward. "And… everything else."

Before I can start for the elevator, he pulls me into his arms and kisses me like I've got all the oxygen in the room.

Our tongues tangle, dance, and I can feel his cock pressing against my pubic bone, right next to where my clit is pulsing.

The elevator door dings, and he pulls away. "Don't worry" is all he says before guiding me to the elevator.

Easy for him to say.

When I walk into work an hour later, everyone is already at their workstations, typing away. I say a quick hello as I set up at my desk, pretending to be all upbeat and casual. Inside, my organs are tying themselves into knots.

I've got a fake coding interview with the most secretive company in the world coming up, I've started an affair... or *something...* with one of the most powerful men in tech, and my brother is still in prison. Oh, and I've got code I need to test and push by the end of this week.

"Hey."

I look up to see January hovering over my desk.

"Yeah?" I make myself bright-eyed.

"You okay?"

I guess I wasn't bright-eyed enough. "Sure."

January's brow wrinkles. "I mean, about the fire last night. At the Gordian construction site."

My face sags. "What? What fire?"

"It's all over the news. You didn't hear anything at your place last night? It's not even a block away."

Oh crap. "Uh... I didn't spend last night at home. What exactly happened?"

January raises an eyebrow but says, "There was a fire at the construction site; the police are saying it's arson. They arrested a homeless man for it."

I turn to my laptop and pull up the local news site. Front and center is the construction site on fire, smoke rising up the steel beams, and next to it, the face of a man I know.

"Oh shit," I mutter. "It's Kevin."

"Kevin? You know him?"

I close my eyes, rub at my forehead. "He's taking care of

Ray's cats. And they think he set fire to the building? On purpose?"

"The police said they had security camera footage of him doing it."

I snap up, my spine going to ice. This is all way too familiar. A homeless man, supposedly caught on a security camera, committing a crime you'd never imagine him doing. "Did they show the camera footage?"

January shakes her head. "I was worried about you when I heard about it this morning. Um… where *did* you stay last night?"

I've got to get Finn into Corvus, got to get to the bottom of this. Kevin's case is related to Ray's. I can just feel it. I take a deep breath, trying to think of a plausible answer that isn't a lie. In the end, I blurt out, "At a hotel. With Finn. But please, can we not talk about it?"

"Sure." January's trying to hide her hurt and confusion, but it's not working. "Did he… Look, I know he's friends with Mark, but I'm always on your side. Did something happen? Something bad?"

I don't think I can love January more than I do right now. She's head over heels for Mark, completely and totally devoted to him… but she looks like she's willing to pop Finn in the nose if he's hurt me.

My smile is shaky but true. "I promise the Finn stuff is…" Oh God, I'm blushing and stammering. "…you know. This news about the fire is upsetting me."

January rubs my arm. "No one got hurt."

Except for Kevin. And I have to make sure the cats will be okay. "Yeah," I say. "At least there's that." I point to my laptop. "I'm going to start testing the new build. We're way behind on that."

"Great." January smiles, then heads back to her own desk.

Instead of running code, I pull up the secure messaging app January wrote, the one Finn sent me the surveillance photos of Ray on. I paste the link to the news story about the arson into a message, then add, *This has to be related. We have to get into Corvus.*

It takes him several hours to message me back, hours that I spend climbing up the walls. And when he does, all he says is *Sit tight. I'm working on it. And memorize the background information I'm sending you.*

So I'm just supposed to wait here for him to do... whatever. Great. Awesome.

But I do. I spend the next three days bouncing out of my skin, memorizing my fake past, trying to work, failing to sleep, and waiting for a signal from Finn. January watches me with worry but doesn't say anything. I want to tell her... but I remember Finn's command to not tell anyone and to keep my mouth shut.

Finn doesn't contact me either. No messages, no emails, no calls—he's not even in our Go forum. No one else in the forum is anywhere near his level, so I log out without playing a single game. I work some on my AI, testing some of the ideas we discussed over dinner, but my heart isn't in it. The suit and the wigs are delivered on the second day, along with the glasses he was talking about. I can't tell what's different about them—other than they're kind of boring—but somehow they're my exact prescription. There's no note with any of it. I don't bother to put on the mermaid wig—I'm too tense to enjoy it.

I'm home on the evening of the third day, in my pajamas and setting out food for Ray's cats. I managed to lure them to my place, but they wouldn't stay inside, not that my roommates would have allowed that. But they will come to the food I leave out.

I also convinced Ray's lawyers to look over Kevin's case, see if they can help him out at all. I'll probably have to sell a kidney—or two—to afford it, but Kevin was Ray's friend. He took care of my brother's cats. I have to do something.

I watch the cats munch on the wet food, eating with one eye on everything going on around them, as if they expect a predator to pounce at any moment. It's a feeling I understand, what with waiting for Finn to contact me.

My phone pings, and I jump right out of my chair. I grab it, fumbling with the buttons as I try to unlock it as fast as I can.

Please be Finn, please be Finn, please be Finn.

I start to sigh with relief when I see a message from him in the secure app but then catch it back when I read the message.

Interview tomorrow. Three p.m. Don't forget the suit.

CHAPTER 17

I don't think I've ever been so nervous in my entire life.

I mean, I probably have at some point, but it's hard to recall when right now. Finn and I are in a hotel room in San Jose, some place middlebrow and nondescript. My interview is in an hour.

Finn called me this morning, told me to take the day off, then meet him here. I was so relieved to hear his voice, but he was brusque, businesslike. The Finn from the hotel was gone, and a stranger was in his place.

The stranger is still here. He's been quizzing me on my fake background from the moment I walked through the door. Even when I was getting changed, he called questions through the bathroom door.

I don't think he's nervous, not like I am—his expression is too impassive, his voice too stern. He just really, really wants this to work. If he could put on the wig and the suit and do this interview himself, he would.

I guess the fantasy's already over then. My heart pinches, but I tell it to behave. I can't be blubbering over a one-night stand when I'm about to walk into the lion's den.

Finn opens his mouth to fire another question at me, but

I hold up my hand. Enough. I don't need this. "What's going on with the glasses?" I tap the eyewear.

The prescription might be correct, but they feel strange, a hair too heavy. I'm going to have to make a conscious effort not to fiddle with them during the interview. Which is in fifty minutes.

Oh God.

"There are tiny infrared lights embedded in the frames, designed to illuminate your face. The human eye can't see the light, but it'll confuse the facial-recognition algos." His jaw might be tensing, but it's hard to tell with the beard. I'd say he's nervous, but I can't see any other signs of it. Maybe he's impatient, annoyed, but Finn doesn't get like that. At least he hasn't with me before.

"Do you think they'll check my glasses at security?"

Finn shakes his head. "People treat glasses like a part of a person's face. They usually don't think to check them, no more than they'd check your eyes or nose."

That makes sense. I only hope it's true.

My phone starts to chime, which means it's time. I have to go.

Finn takes me by the shoulders, his gaze burning into mine. "Remember your name?"

"Stella Riley," I supply automatically.

"Good." His mouth flattens. "You'll do fine. Great. Perfect." He takes a deep inhale, his hands tightening on my shoulders.

And then he's kissing me, brief and fierce, tearing himself away before I can even blink.

"The Uber's waiting," he says, dropping his hands from my shoulders. "I didn't mess up your lipstick."

I touch the corner of my mouth anyway, holding in the feel of him. "Thanks," I say, dazed. "I should be going."

Finn doesn't touch me again as I leave, but I can't stop

thinking about that kiss the entire ride over. What did it mean? Was it for good luck? A goodbye?

Did it mean he can't wait for this Corvus break-in to be over so we can get back to being together?

When I see the Corvus building—nothing but flat, blank glass and a discreet logo at the very top floor—a chill runs through me, chasing away all my questions about the kiss.

But I don't let that show. Instead, I slip into the character of Stella Riley. She wouldn't be frightened; this is the chance she's been waiting for. Nervous, maybe, but it would be a good, determined kind of nervous. I force my anxiety to shape itself to that type of stress.

The security dudes at the front desk are some of the most intimidating guys I have ever seen. I'm guessing that's the point though. I can't really remember if they were here the last time I was in this building, but the last time I was in this building I was more concerned with making sure January didn't sell the company away than taking in the surroundings.

This time I study every detail in case this all goes very, very wrong. Would I be able to reach the front door before one of these guys could tackle me? I honestly don't know. They're big and I'm quick, but this is also their job, tackling people who aren't supposed to be here.

I blink coolly as I hand over my ID. Stella wouldn't be thinking of escape routes.

They look over my ID for what seems like hours, turning it this way and that, taking more care than a bouncer at the strictest bar. Eventually, right when my heart's about to stop, they hand me back my ID and offer me a visitor pass with my name on it. Stella Riley, that's me. The badge has a photo of me they must have taken on my way into the building, which isn't creepy at all.

Stella would be impressed though, so I pretend to be too.

There's a set of unmarked doors at the end of this security nook, the only way in or out that I can see. The doors are so unmarked they don't even have handles; the security guards have to do some magic at their console to open them. It seems to take forever between the moment when they hand me my visitor badge and tell me to enter and when the doors actually open.

Minerva Dyne is waiting for me just beyond the doors.

Oh shit. My heart, my lungs, every nerve comes to a crashing stop.

She knows. It's over. *Fuckfuckfuckfu—*

But then she smiles, not exactly warmly, and holds out her hand. It takes me a moment to restart myself, but then I'm smiling like Stella would, giving Minerva a crisp handshake.

"Stella Riley," I say with polished confidence. "So pleased to be here."

"Minerva." Her eyebrow twitches like she might want to raise it. "I'm Mr. Fuchs's assistant. He's very interested in this particular project, and we've been searching for some time for an appropriate person for it, so I'll be taking the lead on this interview myself."

That's kind of strange, because as far as I know, Minerva isn't a coder, but Stella wouldn't question it, so I don't.

"Great. I'm really looking forward to this." The fact that I can get that out without choking proves I'm quite possibly the world's greatest actress in this moment.

Minerva simply gestures for me to follow her.

The inside of the building is eerie; there's no other way to describe it. There're no signs on any of the doors and sometimes not even handles. And there are literally no people. Not a single soul. It's like something out of a horror movie.

Minerva doesn't make chitchat as she leads me through the hallway, not that I expected her to. There is an itch deep at the base of my neck telling me she knows who I am. She's recognized me and she's leading me into some secure room in order to ritualistically torture me or something.

I try to tell the itch to shut up, that those kinds of thoughts really aren't helping, but it's not listening to me. Stella wouldn't have that itch. I've got to get rid of it before it gives me away.

Finally, finally Minerva stops and opens a door. Or rather she stops in front of the door and it opens automatically at her presence.

Okay, now I'm really freaked out. That kind of security is intense. I'd say it's like Fort Knox, but not even Fort Knox has these kinds of measures.

Inside, a team of about ten engineers wait in a pretty nondescript conference room. For all the craziness of the hallways with the unmarked doors and lack of a way to actually enter them, this conference room is pretty boring. I was expecting something out of James Bond after all the lead-up.

The engineers all look pretty typical, if a little more stressed and exhausted than your average tech guys. I imagine that working for Fuchs is no picnic, even with the high salaries.

Thank God this isn't a real job interview. I already hate this place, and I haven't even been inside five minutes.

But Stella would love it here with all the high-tech security bullshit and the chance to finally see inside Corvus's dungeon. So I put on my widest, most amazing smile and start shaking hands.

I'm introducing myself to Engineer Number Six when a side door opens and Arne Fuchs walks in.

If you didn't know who he was, you'd never guess. He's dressed the same as every other engineer, middle-aged, completely unremarkable. He doesn't introduce himself, no one says anything to him as he sits down, but a current runs through the room. It feels like everyone is sitting on a live wire.

"Whenever you're ready," Minerva says.

I allow myself a deep inhale, because Stella would do the same, then I plunge forward.

Two hours later, I realize why Finn needed me for this particular interview. These guys are basically expecting me to design a simple AI right here in front of them, using only the whiteboard in the conference room. It's not exactly tough or outside my intellectual capacity, but it's still pretty goddamn exhausting. And these guys have absolutely no sense of humor. It's like trying to interact with corpses.

Worst of all is how Fuchs keeps watching me. He hasn't said a word, not a single one to anybody, but he hasn't once taken his eyes off me. Is he doing it to rattle me? Does he suspect something is up? Or is he just that much of a creep?

At minute 136 of this interrogation, I stop, squeeze my eyes shut hard. A headache is starting in my temple, tendrils of pain wrapping around the base of my skull. I'm still not used to these glasses, but there's no way I can take them off. And I can't quit this interview—I've gotten nowhere near the bathroom and haven't seen a good point to stop. They haven't even revealed a single detail of the project I'd be working on, beyond the fact that it involves AI. If it concerns their panopticon project, I have no idea.

Fuchs is still staring at me. I can feel his gaze on my back, right between my shoulders. Like he's mentally aiming for that spot.

I have to finish this. I'm going to give myself away with how nervous and blurry my thoughts are getting. I raise the pen back to the board, ready to finish this explanation… but my brain can't come up with what I meant to say.

Minerva rises then, quickly but smoothly. "I think Ms. Riley needs a break. Let's have some coffee, then come back to this."

I'm so grateful to her I almost forget she's my enemy.

"Great," I say too rapidly. "Where's the ladies' room?"

Finally, finally I can do what I came here to do, then get the fuck out of this place.

"I'll show you," Minerva says.

Oh crap. She can't actually be in the bathroom when I'm destroying the toilet. But I can't think how to gracefully tell her thanks but no thanks. And this might be my only chance to use the bathroom here.

Damn, damn, damn I chant to myself as we walk through the hallway. Minerva stops in front of another unmarked door, this one with a doorknob.

"Right through here," she says. There's something in her expression that snags on me. Like she knows something and is trying to hide it.

I inwardly give myself a shake. That's ridiculous, and I'm being paranoid. Maybe because I want to believe someone in this company isn't horribly and completely evil. But she's not a likely candidate for that role. Nobody gets to be Fuchs's right-hand person, the one he keeps closest, by being secretly good.

We walk in together and each find our own stall. When I shut the stall door, I don't bother to pull my skirt up or my panties down because the stall dividers go all the way to the floor. Thank God for small mercies.

I can hear Minerva shuffling around, two stalls down. She can hear me too then.

I can't decide what to do. Should I just go for it and be as quiet as possible? Or should I wait and hope for another chance?

We're two hours in though, and I'm flagging. If I wait for another chance, I'm likely to blow my cover.

Maybe she'll expect me to find my way back to the conference room on my own. Yes, that would be ideal. I should wait to see if she does that.

She finishes up, and there's the sound of the sink running, the paper-towel dispenser cranking, and then…

Then nothing. She's not opening the door. She's not going out.

She's waiting for me, waiting inside the bathroom.

Every swear word I know floods my brain.

She's never going to leave me alone in this bathroom. She's never going to leave me alone anywhere in this building.

Well, fuck it. It's now or never. I fumble for the plastic bag hidden in the waistband of my panties, tucked in the small of my back. I put it there in case they searched my bag. The bag is half the size of a sandwich baggie, filled with a dark gray powder that looks like cement. Finn didn't explain exactly what it was though.

I'm trying to be as quiet as possible, but every noise sounds horrifyingly loud in the echoing bathroom. But maybe Minerva will think it sounds like me opening feminine hygiene products or something.

I roll my eyes at myself as I try to tug the bag open without a sound. *Feminine hygiene products?* I have never used those words before in my life. This whole thing is really getting to me.

"Everything okay?" Minerva asks.

No, it's not, because the bag's not opening and I'm terrified to pull harder. "Yeah, sorry."

Right as I say that, the bag opens, the noise of it covered up by my voice. Thank God.

Now I have to dump it into the bowl and without Minerva hearing. Which means I should probably make some small talk. I close my eyes. Which I should have been doing all along. I'm such an idiot.

"This place is so amazing," I say, tipping the bag so that only the smallest stream of powder falls into the toilet. "What's it like to work here?"

I sound like a cheerful dunce, but I don't think she can hear what I'm doing.

"It's great," she says so dryly I suspect she might be screwing with me.

"I can imagine." The last of the powder falls into the bowl. I shake the bag for good measure, and some powder smears across my skirt.

Awesome. I've got to get that off my skirt. My heart starts to beat so quickly my hands are shaking in time with it.

This was a terrible, awful idea. This entire thing is a goddamn disaster, and I'm going to kill Finn the second I see him again.

I grab some toilet paper and rub wildly at my skirt, practically beating out the dust. Once it's clean, I toss the toilet paper into the bowl and flush. I do it once more—let Minerva think what she wants—then step back to see my handiwork. Everything looks the same, but according to Finn that stuff I just flushed down the toilet should harden in a few hours. It's going to harden right inside the pipes and completely destroy the plumbing.

When he said break a toilet, I imagined coming in here with a sledgehammer, smashing every porcelain bowl to fragments, water spraying everywhere. This is a much more subtle effect.

After that, I put myself back together, making sure the plastic baggie is retucked securely inside my waistband. That would be a really awful thing to be caught with.

I take a deep breath and close my eyes. Time to be Stella again, the innocent, competent interviewee, a woman who has absolutely nothing to hide and is totally interested in this job.

I open my eyes and open the stall door.

Minerva is waiting there, propped against the wall. She's staring right at my stall. I can't tell if she suspects I was up to something in there or if she *knows* I was up to something in there.

I give her a brief, tight smile, the kind you give any

stranger you come across in the bathroom, and head for the sink. There's still a tiny bit of dust on my palms, and I hope that Minerva hasn't noticed it. I scrub my hands maybe a touch too long, but I have to be certain the dust is gone. Once I'm done, I turn to face her, my face blankly polite.

"Should we head back?" I ask, as if this were any other ordinary interview.

Something flashes across her face, tight and pinched, and then it's gone just as quickly as it came. "Yes. Let's see if we can finish this up."

What she doesn't know is that my job is already done.

CHAPTER 18

I fucking hate this hotel room.

Not because it's not the penthouse at the Fairmont—I've slept in worse hotels than this one and didn't care—but because Doc isn't back yet. It's been over four hours, and I'm about to chew through the drywall.

I can't work, I can't play Go, and I can barely pace. The room's too damn small for me to take more than four steps in any direction. This was a stupid idea, relying way too much on luck. I hate luck. Skill will almost never fail, and Doc's pretty damn skilled, but the thinness of the line between her skills and danger is now really fucking clear to me. Clear enough to make my chest ache.

I started having doubts about this the moment she left our room at the Fairmont. And I never have doubts about my schemes.

Only this time I've involved her. She got nervous, then I got doubts, except I couldn't think of an alternative plan. And now I've fucking sent her into danger.

Stupid Finn. It's one thing to put myself into these kinds of situations, but to put her… I didn't think it would be this bad. This agonizing, waiting for her with nothing to do.

If she isn't back in fifteen minutes, I'm going in after her.

Coding interviews aren't this goddamn long. I'll march in there, grab Fuchs by his skinny chicken neck, and slam him—

My head snaps up as the door handle turns. When Doc walks in, looking nothing like herself, my heart explodes, then reassembles itself.

She stares at me for a long moment, her cheeks pale.

Fuck. She couldn't do it. Goddammit, I was such an idiot, sending her into Fuchs's claws to attempt something so stupid.

Then she smiles wide and slow. "I did it. If they suspected, they never showed it."

In an instant, I've got her in my arms. She doesn't even smell right, and her hair is the wrong color, and I'm going to burn that suit, but I don't care. I'm too relieved.

"Jesus Christ," I mutter into her wig.

"Are you okay?" Her voice is muffled by my chest.

No, I'm not okay. I thought I would be when I saw her, but somehow it's worse. How is it worse? It makes no sense and I don't understand. This is something I've never experienced before.

"I put you in danger." I shake my head, nearly pulling her wig off. "I never should have sent you."

"But I did it. The toilet is broken."

She says that so seriously, so earnestly I have to laugh. "What took you so long?"

Doc tucks her head under my jaw, sighing as she does. "Coding interviews always take forever. They made me design an AI from scratch right there on the whiteboard. Oh, and Fuchs was there."

My entire body goes tight. "He was? What did he say?"

"Nothing. He didn't say a word, just kept staring at me."

If Fuchs was there… Whatever project she was interviewing for had to be important. Really important. "What did they say about the project?"

"Nothing. Not a word. And Minerva was too."

Minerva and Fuchs? Something is definitely up. "Did you catch the names of anyone else?"

Her brow wrinkles. "Sure. I think so."

I maneuver her to the desk and hand her a pen and paper. "Write them all down. I have a feeling we'll see those names in whatever we pull out of Corvus."

Doc starts to scribble. "Do you even know what to look for when you get in?"

When, not if. She doesn't have any more doubts about this scheme. I put her in danger, but she still believes. I swallow down my guilt at that. "Grace told me the code name of the surveillance group: Oracular. I'll look for that."

"Oracular?" She bites her lip as she tries to remember a name. "That's not a great code name."

"Well, they're claiming they can use AI and surveillance to predict who'll be a criminal. And Fuchs has always had a flair for the dramatic."

She sets the pen down. "That's all of them." She looks up at me, wearing those glasses that aren't hers, her wig tilted, but looking so confident in spite of it. "What happens next?"

I make my own trip inside Corvus. Everything's ready; they just need to call in the maintenance company. I'm betting it will be tomorrow at the latest.

Doc doesn't need to worry about that though. She's done her part and done it beautifully.

"First," I say, easing off the glasses, "we get you out of this crap. And into the tub."

She does that sigh of hers. "How did you know I needed to wash that place off?"

Because somehow I just *know* her. I can't explain it—everything else I know, which is a lot, I had to study. To practice.

Doc came to me without any of that, which makes her even more special. Once this is over, I'm going to have to

take a long, hard look at what happens after, at what I want
to be with her. I want... well, I want to be with her. Just
her, for as long as I can. *Forever,* a small voice says
inside me.

Which scares the shit out of me, because what if she
doesn't feel the same?

I shake that off. For now I need to take care of her. I put
her in danger, and I need to make it up to her.

I pull off the wig and toss it aside. Her hair is under a cap
that's pinned down; I make short work of it, letting her
natural hair fall free again. Only, it's kinked and matted from
its time under wraps.

I'll fix that for her in the bath.

I hold up one finger. "Wait here. I'll get it ready."

She tucks her bare feet under herself—she's lost those
awful shoes somewhere—and gives me a sweet smile that
hits me right in the chest. "I'm not going anywhere."

Once I'm in the bathroom, I turn the taps on full. I dump
in some bath gel until the water smells fluffy and flowery,
suds rising almost over the tub lip. It's going to make a huge
mess when Doc gets in, but whatever. I want this to be the
best bath of her life even if it's in a decidedly mediocre-hotel
bathroom.

She's waiting right where I left her when I come back. I
take her hand and pull her up out of the chair and toward
me. As I do, she hooks an arm around my neck and lifts her
face for a kiss.

"Was that why you were so cold before?" she asks
between kisses. "Because you were afraid?"

Afraid. My body instinctively rejects the word. I've never
been afraid in my entire life. Not me, not Finn the Badass.

But she's right. I was scared for her. Which was probably
why I was an ass earlier. She's way too smart, reads me way
too easily. Which scares me all over again.

"Yes." I press my mouth to her hairline, her temple, the

bridge of her nose. "When you walked through that door... You don't know how that felt."

"But I will." She leans back, the better to look up at me. "When you go in."

Fuck. She doesn't need to worry about that. I'm a pro at that. "Don't." I lift her into my arms and start for the bathroom. "Don't even give it another thought."

"But I won't be able to help it."

I set her down, making sure her feet land on the rug and not the cold tile. I know exactly how to distract her from thinking about my trip into Corvus. With a quick flick of my arms, I've got the suit jacket off. I find the button on her skirt and simply tear it off. When it falls to the floor, I kick it into a corner along with the jacket.

"That wasn't cheap," she says, but she's smiling.

"Did you really want to wear that again?"

"No."

She helpfully lifts her arms as I pull off her shirt. And then I have to take a minute to admire her bra and panties. The suit and blouse might have been completely unlike her, but underneath is stuff that just screams Doc. They match, of course, and they're in a pale purple almost the same shade as her hair. They're not made of lace but tulle held together by purple and yellow strips of fabric. It's cute and flirty and funky all at once.

I've seen lots of lingerie designed specifically to ignite lust before, but nothing hits me harder than those scraps of fabric across the curves I'm dying to touch.

But I keep my hands slow, reverent, as I reach for the clasp of her bra. I want to make her feel cherished this time. To let her know how much what she did means to me.

The clasp comes open as if it were just waiting for my hands. Her breasts are even more beautiful without the bra, her nipples dark and pouty. My hands want to tremble, want to test the firmness of her nipples, but I force them to be quiet. I sneak a kiss at the border of her areolas since I can't resist that. Her skin is smooth, faintly cool, and my pulse kicks.

I step back, help her out of her panties. Her legs are dizzyingly long, and where they lead…

The sight of the dark curls between her legs has me swallowing hard. *Down, boy.*

I take her hand and help her into the tub, the perfect gentleman. I'm not, of course, but I'll pretend for her right now.

This moment is completely for her.

CHAPTER 19

When I sink into the tub, I have to moan. The water is the perfect temperature, and it smells like heaven, if it were made of bath soaps. The last bit of anxiety lingering at the base of my skull unknots and floats away.

I slide all the way down until I'm completely submerged, my hands pushing to keep me under. There's nothing but floaty warmth where I am.

Eventually I bob back up, water streaming through my hair and down my face. As it does, I feel Stella draining away with it. I don't have to be her ever again, thank goodness.

Finn is smiling at me. "You looked like a mermaid."

"Lucky for you I don't have a tail." I push my hair out of my eyes. "Unless fish tails are a kink of yours?"

"If you had a fish tail, yes." He reaches for a bottle of shampoo on the tub's edge. "Don't worry; it's color safe."

He begins to massage the shampoo into my hair, his fingers rubbing slow, hypnotic circles on my scalp. I close my eyes and let him go to town.

This is a side of Finn I haven't seen yet, this tender, caring man. Not that he was mean before, but taking care of me like this… It's doing a number on my heart. This is exactly what I need after that interview, and he knew it even before I did.

"Did you bring the Go board?" I ask sleepily. First I want to break in the hotel bed—it's a king, so why not?—then I want to match wits against him.

"No." His voice is lower than usual. "We can play at my place later."

"I have to say your bathroom looks amazing, but this is the best bath I've ever had."

He lifts his hands from my hair, and I open my eyes. "Sit up and tilt your head back." He takes one of the little plastic cups that was by the ice bucket and uses it to rinse my hair, massaging all the shampoo out.

"Where did you learn to do this?" This is better than some washes I've had at salons.

"You have to learn how to wash hair?" He's opening a conditioner bottle now. "Like, at a special school?"

"Well, I don't know if you have to go to school, but shampooer is a position at certain salons."

He shakes his head as he squirts some conditioner into his palm. It's thick and rich, the kind I privately call "bear-fat conditioner." The man knows his hair products.

As he combs the conditioner through my hair with his fingers, I let my head fall back, savoring this pampering. I feel completely like myself again, only better. More relaxed.

"We should've gone back to my place," he says conversationally. "My shower will spray you from three hundred and sixty degrees. And there are showerheads at hip height too."

He lets my imagination work on that, at where exactly that stream of water would be directed. I wouldn't even have to worry about holding the shower nozzle.

"Yeah, we definitely need to go back to your place." I tilt my head so he can comb through the hair over my ears. I don't think I've ever had someone do my hair so gently, not even my mom.

"Head back."

The water sluices through my hair, down my back, along

my shoulders. Everything is washed away except for sensation. The warmth of the water, the lingering tingles in my scalp, the scent of the shampoo, the sound of his breathing.

When he's done, I keep my eyes closed because I'm too relaxed to open them. "Are you going to scrub me down now?"

His laugh is low and rough. "I like you dirty. No, no scrubbing—but I am going to play with you."

Oh, I do like the sound of that. But I want to play with him too. So I grab the front of his shirt and pull him down to me. The water swells over the edge of the tub, sloshing across the floor and soaking his knees. Good. We're both wet now.

If he notices, it doesn't stop him from kissing me deeply. In fact, it feels like he might be smiling against my mouth.

"You couldn't even let me get undressed first?"

I tighten my grip on his shirt. "Are you complaining?"

"Hell, no." With both arms, he reaches into the tub, getting soaked up to his shoulders, and lifts me out. We're both dripping like crazy onto the floor, and I kind of love it.

As he carries me into the main room, I snag a towel from the rack. The bed's definitely going to get messy, but at least we can contain some of it.

"This bed is crap," he mutters as he looks down at it. "We should have just gone back to my place."

"Oh, we'll fuck there too."

The heat in his expression threatens to singe my eyebrows off. "Holy Christ, you're perfect."

Perfect. A man's never called me that before. Not like this, like I'm the answer to all his dreams.

Unless... unless Finn has called other women perfect before. This is heat of the moment and all that.

Before I can ponder it more, he's tossing me onto the bed. I roll the towel under me as quick as I can, just so the bed isn't soaked.

He strips off his clothes, tossing them into a pile. It's cute how careless he is about it—he's not putting on a show, he just wants the damn things off. Wants to be naked with me.

I shiver and not from the cold. He wants me so much, as much as I want him. That's some heady, dizzying stuff.

He crawls up over me, closing me in with his big heat. We kiss, long and slow, dreamlike. I'm still a little woozy from the bath, and it feels like he's getting a little woozy too, that he's falling into this waking dream with me.

Our hands are busy, running over skin—his hands on me, mine on him. His hair is coarse, his muscles are like steel, and his skin is molten silk. His hands make my skin feel like silk too, make my muscles melt and my pussy clench.

"You remembered the condoms, right?" If he's forgotten them, I'm revoking his genius status immediately.

He pulls open the bedside drawer, revealing at least four boxes of Trojan Magnums. Phew. His genius status is safe.

His hand comes back to me, settling in the small of my back and pulling me upright. He arranges us so that I'm in his lap, straddling his thighs, spread wide for him. It's painfully intimate, almost more so than my being on top or beneath him. We're completely face-to-face; there's nowhere to look but at each other.

His cock juts between us, thick and flushed deep red. The crown is nearly purple.

"Is your brain still getting oxygen?" I ask.

He laughs, once, short. "Not as much as usual. Don't worry, I won't pass out. I can think with this head just as good as the other one."

Now it's my turn to laugh. As I do, his hand slips between my folds. My laugh gets caught in a gasp because I'm so wet for him, and all we've done is kiss.

It was the bath. It was the shampooing. It was the tenderness.

He finds my clit, stroking it. His touch is knowing, expert —he's learned the secrets of me so quickly.

I can only look into his eyes as he works me into an orgasm. He looks… amazed. At me. And maybe at himself, that he can bring me to this point, on the edge of the most incredible pleasure. He's a genius, made scads and scads of money—but this is what amazes him.

It's his expression that sends me over the edge. I come with a clench and a moan, then another, my climax flowing over me like the water escaped the tub, uncontainable.

When I can see again, he's already rolling one of the condoms on. I rise up on my knees, our hands meeting at the base of his cock as we match his angle to mine. Then I sink down on him.

There's nothing like the fullness I feel when he's inside me, deep. It's beyond complete. I roll my hips, searching out that friction. He pumps, slow and long, pulling out until I'm just ready to protest, then thrusting into me until I'm stretched almost too far to bear. The contrasts drive me wild, have my hips bucking.

I sigh, and his control breaks right down the middle. No more teasing thrusts—he's driving into me, and I'm meeting him stroke for stroke. His pelvis is catching my clit, grinding on it, and it's already sensitized from my earlier orgasm. Every touch is a zap of pure lightning.

I bite my lower lip hard. "*Fuuuuck.*" His shoulders are like iron under my hands, bunching against my nails with each thrust.

My tits are bouncing, my thighs are burning, and my pussy is so slick I can hear us moving together. This is dirty, frantic sex—but with *eye contact*—and I love it. Adore it.

This is the kind of sex I want to have for the rest of my life.

My orgasm this time isn't anything like water; it's sharp

and bright, a dagger of sensation. It twists in my core so hard my vision goes blank.

But I feel his cock swelling in my pussy, can hear his grunts as he pumps quick and fierce into me, sense his muscles tightening, then releasing as he comes, spilling deep inside me.

We're still upright, still clinging to each other, but we're sweaty and limp now, propped against each other. His forehead is touching mine, our breath sawing in and out in unison. We're sticky and loose, and the towel under us is wet and cold on my ass… but it's perfect.

I shift, trying to bring some blood back to my hips. There's an ominous creaking from the bed frame.

"Is that—"

There's a sharp crack, and then we're falling half a foot. My teeth snap together when we hit bottom.

We blink at each other.

"I think we broke the bed," I say, quietly shocked.

"I think we did too," he says, just as quiet.

And then we start to laugh so hard that tears stream out of my eyes.

"Oh my God," I gasp out. "The poor housekeepers. We'll have to leave them a massive tip."

"Fuck it," Finn says. "I'll buy the whole hotel. Problem solved."

"Really?"

"After what we did to this room?" He looks toward the bathroom, then bounces on the bed. "Yeah, I have to."

I lay my head against his chest and listen to him breathe for a moment. "We should get out of here before we do any more damage."

"Definitely. But if we break my bed, I'm going to be pissed."

The laughter in his voice tells me he won't be. Not really.

CHAPTER 20

The second phase of our plan is going into effect today.

I pull on the overalls I'm borrowing from my brother-in-law since he's the only person in the family who's close to me in size. Also, his overalls are pretty realistically broken in. There's paint on the knee, frayed cuffs, and a worn spot where he probably set his hip against an engine and burned the fabric. He's a mechanic, not a plumber, but I doubt those pampered brats at Corvus know the difference. To them, all working-class dudes look alike, aren't worth their attention, and are barely smarter than their office dogs.

But I know the working-class people I grew up with aren't dumb—they're just as smart as those coders at Corvus. It's only luck, an accident of birth that put the Corvus guys where they are and kept the working-class guys where they are. It's why I hate luck even though luck has gotten me where I am too.

Doc comes into my bedroom just as I'm zipping up the overalls. When she sees me, she does a double take, and then her expression falls.

"You... You..." It's all she can get out as she gestures wildly at me.

"What?" I run my hands down the front of the overalls. "I swear they're clean. They just don't look it."

She still gestures wordlessly at me.

I run my hand across my face to tug my beard. As my fingers find bare skin, I remember and curse under my breath.

"Is it the beard?" I ask. "Because it had to go if I was gonna be unrecognizable."

While I didn't cry while I was shaving it off, my throat did get kind of tight. And my eyes burned a bit. But I didn't fucking *cry.*

"I'm sorry, it's just so shocking." She puts her fingers to her lower lip. "I've never seen any pictures of you without a beard."

"Yeah, I've never not had it. As soon as I got facial hair, I grew one." There are some pictures of me without a beard, but I hate it when people see those. Which Mark and Logan took advantage of when they sent some to be printed in *Wired*, the assholes. "It feels pretty weird to be without one, but you do what you have to do."

Doc chews on her lower lip, her eyes pinched. "Well, it'll grow back. Right?"

It should, but it's going to be pretty goddamned itchy as I wait for it to grow out, and I hate the way I look without it. I'm not ashamed of my scars, but the one running along my jaw brings too many stares for my peace of mind. Everybody likes to ask about it too, but it's a pretty boring story. I went head over heels in an ATV when I was eight and busted the underside of my jaw straight open. I had to have my jaw wired shut afterward. My parents have always hated talking about that, probably because I scared the shit out of them that day, so I try not to bring it up.

There's a lot about my childhood that I try not to bring up.

Doc doesn't ask about the scar, and I can't tell if she's

staring at it or my general lack of beard. At least the scar will make me unrecognizable to everybody working at Corvus. A plumber with no beard and a massive scar—definitely not me. Their minds won't be able make the leap.

Doc's gaze runs from my head to my feet and then back up again. "You're going in as maintenance man? It's pretty fucking ballsy of you."

I grin at her. "Ballsy is my middle name. I need to be able to actually get inside the building, and this was the only way I could think to do it." I had to practically be invisible, and who's more invisible than the maintenance staff?

Her face screws up in a frown. "The disguise is good, but do you really think they're going to let you just waltz up and touch a machine? They wouldn't even let me go to the bathroom by myself."

"But they thought you had enough knowledge to be dangerous. They won't think that about me. Nobody's going to stay to watch me root around in the plumbing system for hours on end."

"You should've been a psychologist," she says. "Or a sociologist or whoever studies stuff like that."

"The social engineering part has always been the most important part of a hack. And I've got a few other tricks to get inside."

The gleam in her eyes is admiring. "I bet you do." Her mouth turns down. "Well, good luck."

I pull her in for a kiss. It's different, kissing her without a beard. I can get closer, more intimate, skin touching skin. Maybe I shouldn't regrow it.

When I release her, Doc does her sigh. "Man, I already miss your beard."

"I'll be back in a few hours. Don't worry about me."

She rolls her eyes. "You can't tell me what to do. You should go. The sooner you leave, the sooner you can come back."

I kiss her one last time. "For luck." And then I force myself to walk out.

I've borrowed a van from the maintenance company, and I take that now to Corvus. I make myself calm, easy—this is just another job, one more toilet to fix in a long line of them. I don't even know what this company does. Something with computers? Whatever.

It must have worked, because security waves me right through without a pat down, without going through my toolbox, although they do give me a visitor pass. Very, very sloppy. They've gotten complacent here.

Once I'm inside, I try not to laugh. The last time I was here, I didn't quite take in the ridiculous, cosmetic security theater. All of it is just so over the top: the unlabeled doors, the lack of doorknobs, the security guards' show out front. Most of this to impress upon people this place is really impenetrable rather than making it so.

Another security guy meets me inside. "It's this way." He starts walking.

He simply assumed I was here to fix the bathroom. Again, this is sloppy. I should have credentials, a background check, my stuff searched, at the minimum. All this is working in my favor, but I still can't help but be irritated by it.

We come to another unmarked door. This one at least has a doorknob. "Here it is." The security guy holds open the door but doesn't walk inside. "The thing just started flooding yesterday and wouldn't stop. I think there's something in the pipe."

Yep, there certainly is. I nod my thanks. "I'll take a look, get this thing fixed right up."

And just as I expected, the security guard takes off.

I smile to myself as I get to work. He was clearly uncomfortable about going into a women's bathroom. That's the thing about human beings, a lot of times they can't get over their own taboos in order to do what they know is necessary.

He knows he should keep an eye on me, should never let me be alone in this place, but he also really, really doesn't want to be in the women's bathroom even if it's empty. It's just a bridge too far, so he has to commit the cardinal sin of leaving me alone.

Not that I'm complaining.

I wait until I hear his footsteps die away, then I wait five minutes more. The entire time there's no other sounds in the hall. It's almost as if this place is empty.

But I know it's not. Thanks to the map Grace drew for me, I know exactly where I need to go. She didn't know much about the specifics of the Oracular division, but she did know where it was. That's really all I need. I can take care of the rest on my own.

I tuck my visitor pass behind the broken toilet. Slowly, quietly, I open the bathroom door. There's nobody in the hallway. I step out, grabbing my toolbox as I do. If they'd bothered to search it, they might have found the false bottom where I keep all the electronics. They think this business of not putting handles on the doors is going to keep somebody out, but I know better.

I make my way down the hall, not going too slow, not going too fast, like I know exactly where I'm going. Like I definitely belong in the more secure areas.

I count down the number of doors in the hall—one, two, three, four, five. I come to an intersection and turn left. I start counting doors again. This time I stop at the third door. It's one of the handleless ones, completely ordinary.

But this is the way into the secure areas of Corvus.

I open the toolbox, get into the false bottom, and pull out my scrambler. It's no bigger than a cell phone, and it knows the exact frequency to tell this door to open up and let me in. Doorknobs or not, they're not keeping me out.

The scrambler whirrs and clicks, which is totally unnecessary, but I like having the illusion of sound to tell me something's happening. One of the perks of designing the device yourself is that you can make it answer to whatever quirks you might have. And I like noises and flashing lights.

The door snicks open in under five seconds.

Bingo.

The door opens into another hallway, this one just as featureless as the last.

I start counting doors again—one, two, three, four, five, six—then open another door with my scrambler. After doing that a couple of times, I start to feel like a rat in a maze, which is probably the whole intention. Not only would it keep intruders out, but it also makes the employees feel nice and despairing. Abandon all hope; there's no way out of here. Real fucking cheery.

After six minutes in the maze, I start to see some signs of life. Behind one door I can hear a faint humming, like an air conditioner going. It's probably the climate-control system. If their server farms are as big as Grace described, it has to take a lot of effort to keep those machines cool.

I count more doors, go down more halls until I finally arrive at the place I need to be. I haven't met another living soul, which I'm grateful for but I'm also oddly freaked out by. There should be some people here. It can't just be machines, featureless doors, and security guards.

When I get to the door I want, it takes the scrambler a really long time to open it. Several minutes, in fact. Security on this room is a lot tighter than anywhere else—which means I've found exactly what I'm looking for. I keep one eye out as the scrambler does its work, looking up and down the hallway. Nothing and nobody appears. I might be the last man on earth, considering how empty this place is.

When the door finally swings open, I do a silent fist pump. This is turning out to be way easier than I thought, so easy that I'm contemptuous of Fuchs. He's one of the most paranoid guys in the business, and this is how he handles his security? It's just way too easy.

The door opens into a massive server farm, which is exactly what I was expecting. There're a couple of terminals at desks, but mostly the room is empty. Somebody should be down here keeping an eye on things, but fortunately nobody wants to work in the server farm. It's too cold and lonely and mind-numbing, which works out perfectly for me.

I sit down at one of the terminals and fire up the machine. With a few keystrokes, I'm inside. Whoever had this open last made sure to log out, but they left a bunch of windows open that they shouldn't have. People get lazy, click on links they shouldn't, use passwords that are easily remembered. And that's how people like me slip inside. Being a great hacker isn't always about knowing the most about code. It's also just waiting for that one moment when people slip up and let you waltz right in.

I start searching for anything labeled Oracular. Soon enough I've got a huge list of files to copy. So I unzip the fly of my overalls and pull out my dick.

If anyone finds me like this, it's going to be real fucking awkward to explain, even beyond my being where I shouldn't be. But I knew I could be searched at the door, and I knew I had to get a USB drive in somehow, so I taped it to the underside of my dick. If there's one guarantee in this world, it's that most people will never touch a stranger's junk even if it's part of their job description. Just like with the bathroom, I took full advantage of squeamishness to get ahead.

As I pull the tape off, I bite back a yelp. Goddamn, but that hurts. And I have to tape it back into place once I'm done. And then pull it off again. I close my eyes and try not to think about it. I take a deep breath and pull off the last bit of tape.

My eyes snap open and my mouth releases a silent scream.

The things I do to get this stuff. I take the tape off the USB drive and try not to think about how much of my skin is stuck to it. Before I can put the key in and start copying, I need to disable the copy prevention system—I'm sure they've got one on here to prevent someone from doing exactly what I'm about to.

Once that's done, I pop the key into the back of the tower and start the copying process. The little pop-up window tells me the download will take five minutes. I start to pace, silently demanding the download rate to hurry up, hurry up, hurry the fuck up.

This is the worst part of the entire thing. Even though I'm not any more exposed than I was before, sneaking through the hallways, I feel like a sitting duck.

If anyone's monitoring this machine, they'll see I'm downloading from it. And then they'll come down to see what's going on or worse, kill the download remotely, and I'm fucked.

Hurry, hurry, hurry. There's a noise from the hallway, a whisper of *something*, and I resist the urge to smack the tower. Whacking a machine might feel good, but it never fixed anything. And maybe I'm hearing things at this point. Christ, I felt less exposed with my dick out earlier.

Finally, finally, the download hits the magic number—one hundred percent!—and finishes. I grab the stick out of the back—thank God for PCs, there's no fucking around with unmounting a USB like on a Mac—and then I tape the key back to the underside of my dick. I tuck everything away, zip up, and head for the exit.

My heart's going a mile a minute as I retrace my steps through the maze. I focus on my breathing, making sure my thoughts stay straight. I might have gotten the information I needed, but if I get lost here, I'm still fucked. To keep myself from flipping out, I imagine what Doc will say when I show her the USB drive. And what we'll find once we start digging into the data I've grabbed. God, I've waited so long to break into Corvus—this is going to be better than any Christmas I've ever had.

I finally make it back into the main hallway just as sweat starts to trickle down my back. At least I have an excuse to be sweaty—plumbing is hard work. It's only going to help with my disguise.

I aim toward the women's bathroom, triumph sizzling through my veins. I've almost done it. I'm almost home free.

And then Minerva Dyne appears around the corner.

Oh fuck. Of all the fucking people to see me…

She stops dead when she sees me, suspicion crinkling her features. "Who are you?"

My heart is hammering in my ears. I point to the name stitched on my overalls, trying to look dumb. "Tom. I'm the plumber."

"Shouldn't you be in the bathroom then?" Her gaze is too tight on me, and it's making my skin crawl. She doesn't recognize me—she'd scream bloody murder if she did—but she clearly knows something is up. "And why aren't you wearing your visitor pass?"

"I left it in the bathroom with my tools. Stuff like that tends to fall into places it shouldn't."

Her mouth flattens. "You have to wear it all the time. I don't care if it gets in the way. And why aren't you in the bathroom?"

"I had to take a piss," I say, enjoying the distaste that flashes across her face.

I'm being deliberately crude, the better to distract her from her suspicions. She'd expect a plumber to be this shitty.

"I see." She makes the *s* sharp with disbelief. "I'll walk you back."

She marches me to the women's bathroom, but she

doesn't come inside. Again, there's that natural taboo. It's her bathroom, she has every right to be there, but I've invaded it. It's not safe for her anymore, so she's not coming inside.

Once she shuts the door behind her, I start banging on the pipes and do some plunging of the toilet. I'm not really doing anything useful, but I wanted her to think I am. If she's not waiting behind that door, listening to me, I'll eat that USB drive.

After about twenty minutes of that—I hope she enjoyed the show—I dump a packet of powder down the toilet, then flush. This is the antidote to what Doc had put in before and will completely dissolve what's in there. It'll be like the toilet was never broken.

I flush a couple more times just for effect and do one last check that I haven't permanently fucked up the toilet. Everything looks nice and swirly. So I gather up my things and saunter back outside.

Minerva's out there waiting for me, just as I expected.

"Who are you with again?"

I hold up my ID tag. "Advanced Building Maintenance. I've been here before fixing stuff. You don't remember me?"

She raises one thinly plucked eyebrow. "No," she says shortly, "I don't."

"Well, I'm all finished in there. It's good as new if you want to give it a try."

"No, thank you," she says coolly. "I'll show you to the front."

She walks me all the way to the security desk. They snatch guilty looks at her as they pat me down like they should have done at the very beginning. They also go through my toolbox but never find the false bottom. And of course they never get near my crotch.

"He's clean," the main security dude says.

"Hmm." Minerva crosses her arms. "If you say so."

I flash her a blank smile, then head for the door. She follows.

Shit. I've got to turn up the charm here to get her off my back.

"Hey," I say, casual as anything, "do you want to get drinks sometime? Maybe dinner? I can give you my number."

She's appalled at the very suggestion. "No, I'm making sure you know your way out."

"Really? I thought maybe you wanted to ask me out since you're following me."

She stops dead and cocks her head. She looks like a snake sighting a mouse moving through the grass. I don't know what I've done to give myself away, but she's on to me. "What did you say your name was again?"

"Tom O'Grady." Ordinary plumber-type name.

"Right. And you said you've been here before?"

"Yep. Another toilet to fix, only it was a different one."

If she checks that story, she'll see that it's true. I made sure to pull up the records of the maintenance company's visits to this building so I would have a plausible cover story if I needed to lie my way out.

"I remember that," she says, "but I don't remember you."

"Do you usually remember the guy who fixes your toilet? Or empties your trash? Or waxes the floors?"

She flushes with embarrassment, which I wasn't expecting. She always struck me as a snob through and through.

"I'm sorry to have kept you," she says stiffly. "Have a nice day."

I let myself whistle as I walk out to my van. After all, it's what a plumber would do.

CHAPTER 21

Waiting for Finn to come back is even more nerve-racking than my coding interview.

I'm pacing in his living room—it's big enough that I can really work up some speed—trying not to think up worst-case scenarios. Which is silly, because what are they gonna do to him, take him to some secure facility and torture him? He's one of the richest, most famous men in the Valley. At worst they'll call the cops, and then he'll talk his way out of it.

But what if he doesn't? What if he's arrested and convicted? And sent away, just like Ray?

I shake out my hands, increase my pace. This is ridiculous. Why am I so anxious about this, inventing stories that will never happen just so I can worry about them?

Because I'm worried about *him*. The realization hits me with a cold shock, stopping me dead. I mean, of course I'm worried about him, but really I'm worried about *him*. Because I like him. In a warm and fuzzy, you-make-my-heart-happy-I-want-to-spend-time-with-you kind of way. A romantic way.

Oh hell. I wasn't supposed to fall for him. I have more

than enough trouble in my life—why am I doing this to myself?

I rub my hands over my face, my cheeks cold beneath my palms. Maybe I never had any choice. I've never felt like this about anyone before—like I'm strapped to a roller coaster I can't control but I'm also having the time of life while also being terrified out of my wits. It's head spinning.

This line of thought is making me crazy; I need to think of something else. Obsessing over how I feel about him isn't going to solve anything.

I catch sight of the Go board, the pieces still left from the game we were playing last night. We went for hours and decided to leave the rest for later. Finn's ahead by several points, but I can see a way to nullify his advantage and take it for my own. Although maybe it's not fair for us to keep playing this game. I've been staring at the board all day, thinking up strategies, and he's been breaking into Corvus, stealing their data and fixing their toilets.

I sink down onto one of the cushions, my attention caught by the game board. Finn really is a great player, and he'd be deadly if he would just settle down and focus on long-term strategy. But maybe he doesn't want to. Maybe he's perfectly happy with the way he plays. And the way he lives.

God, that's a depressing thought.

I start to pick up the pieces and put them in their proper bowls. I've suddenly lost my taste for beating him in this match. I only want him to come back, safe and sound.

When the front door finally opens, I nearly jump out of my skin. This isn't my house, and while I'm supposed to be here, it still feels weird to hear a strange front door open when I'm all alone.

When Finn appears in the doorway, I sigh with relief. "Are you okay?" I ask. "Did they catch you? Did anything happen?"

He smiles his arrogant smile. "You don't want to know what I got first?"

I roll my eyes. "I'm sorry I was concerned about you. I won't let it happen again."

"No, it was nice. You should definitely do it again."

My breath gets caught in my throat. Is he asking for something more? Or is this more of his flirty teasing? "I'm not going to get many opportunities after this, am I?" I ask with painful casualness.

He goes still, for so short a moment I almost miss it. "Well," he says, as casual as I was, "we might pull off another heist in the future. You never know."

Oh. My breath whispers out of me, then gets caught on the lump in my throat. He... This sounds like he's talking about us being together in this hypothetical future. He's being offhand about it, but I think that's his way of protecting himself when things get deep.

Which means... things are deep. For him and for me.

I wet my lips, thinking about how to answer him without spooking him. "Maybe," I say, letting some of my feelings for him leak into that. "We make a pretty good team."

A look pulses between us, heavy with emotion and more than a dash of lust. Oh boy. Oh boy, oh boy, oh boy, what are we doing here? Is it what I think we are?

Then he grimaces and the atmosphere dissolves. He looks like he's hurting.

"Are you okay?" I walk over to him, imagining the security goons working him over and leaving bruises everywhere. "You haven't told me what happened."

He shifts uncomfortably. "Everything went fine. I got in with no issues, got the data, and fixed the toilet. I ran into Minerva though."

"Oh no." I put my hand over my mouth. That's bad. She saw me, she saw him—she's going to know something's up.

Finn shrugs. "She seemed suspicious, but I think she

treats everyone that way. At any rate, they never found the USB drive."

"Where *is* the drive?"

A strange look crosses his face. "I've gotta go into the bathroom to get it."

My mouth drops open.

"It's just taped to my dick," he says.

I blink at him. "The USB drive… is taped… to your *penis?*"

He guffaws. "Yep. I figured that was one place they wouldn't check."

Heat rises in my cheeks. "Didn't that hurt?"

"Like a bastard," he agrees cheerfully. "But maybe I can find someone to kiss it better."

The air between us goes hot and thick. I'm imagining kissing his cock, rubbing my lips over it, the skin smooth and hot, and I can tell he's imagining the exact same thing. It's like our hearts are meeting as our minds twirl out the same fantasy.

"I think," I say weakly, "you could probably find someone. You're a handsome guy." I'm trying to make a joke, mostly out of habit, but it doesn't land.

"I don't want just anyone." He's wearing a seriousness I've never seen on him before. Or maybe it's just the lack of a beard—he can't hide his expressions behind it anymore.

And then he winces again and the moment is gone.

"I'm sorry, but I've got to get this off," he says. "I'm not going to have any skin left on my dick if I don't."

"Eww."

"Never say that hacking isn't physically dangerous."

"You're definitely a martyr for the cause."

He shifts again. "Ouch. Once I get this off and dunked in some hand sanitizer, we're taking off."

I frown. "Taking off? For where? The secure facility?" That seems the best place to start sifting through what we've grabbed.

"Nope. I'm gonna need to do some serious thinking on this if there's encryption to crack, so we're going to my place in Baja. The jet's already waiting at SFO." He says it offhandedly, like it's no big deal to just leave the country on a whim.

"I can't… There's work, and I don't even have my passport."

"I already cleared it with January and sent my assistant to pack a bag for you and grab your passport."

Someday his tendency to arrange everything without telling me is going to really, really annoy me. But not today. Suddenly all I can think of is pristine beaches and fresh ocean-caught fish and taking all the time in the world to dig into that data.

"You talked to January?" I ask. "What did she say?"

God, she probably giggled the whole time, thinking we're going on a sex trip. Which… there's likely to be sex and a lot of it, so she's not wrong.

"I asked pretty please could I borrow you for this project I'm working on. She said fine."

I'm betting she said more. I guess I'll hear about it when we get back.

"When is the plane supposed to leave?" I ask. "I need to make sure someone feeds the cat."

"The plane leaves when I tell it to. So take your time." With that, he disappears into his secret hallway.

The plane leaves when I tell it to. Everything arranges itself the way he wants it to, and I suddenly have a bright realization—he'll arrange for Ray's release with this data. Because he'll will it into being.

Maybe falling for him wasn't such a bad idea. Maybe if he can will a happy ending for Ray into being, he can do the same for us.

I look outside the jet window and frown. "This doesn't look anything like Baja. This is…"

I don't let the rest of that out because I can hardly believe it. It can't be true. Finn wouldn't bring me here, not when we have to crack open the data he got from Corvus.

My hand on the window frames the dry, flat plain that flows seamlessly from the airstrip. It looks so familiar, but I never knew there was an airport. We always had to drive out here, almost six hours of unremitting boredom.

"Rancho Carne?" He gestures to the stewardess, who hurries over with a hot towel. "That's because it is. I thought you might want to visit Ray, and it's on our way to Mexico."

It's only on our way because we're flying on a private jet. This place isn't on the way to anywhere.

"I can't believe it." I keep my hand on the window, cold and hard. I'm going to see Ray. I can ask him about the cameras, the police framing him, Corvus tracking him even before he was accused. With whatever he can give me and whatever we can get from the Corvus data, we'll prove his innocence. They'll have to let him out.

"Believe it," Finn says, rising out of his seat and offering me his hand. "The car's already waiting on the runway."

But the car waiting for us isn't a car. It's a truck. I'm no truck expert, but it seems very new and very nice, with shining chrome wheels and bumpers. Finn himself drives us out of the airport and into his hometown.

"This is where you grew up," I say as I take in the outskirts. There's a huge athletic facility here, brand-new with acres of sparkling green grass. "Huh, I wonder when this got put in."

"Six months ago." He's not exactly relaxed as he drives us down the main strip, but I can't quite put my finger on what he's feeling. His hands are tapping too fast against the wheel.

"Everything okay?"

"Fine." He bites off the word.

Clearly he's not, but maybe he's got bad memories of this place. So I steer the conversation to something more innocent. "I wonder how they got the money for this park."

He says nothing at all.

Main Street appears then, filled with faded stucco storefronts… and a huge, gleaming library right in the middle of them. It's smaller than the athletic park but just as new.

"Wow." I tap the window as it goes past. There's no donor name on it, but someone must have given the money for it. The state is too broke to be handing out funds for this kind of stuff, not for a place as small and out of the way as Rancho Carne.

I look over at Finn, who's still drumming the wheel. He's glancing around like he's worried about being recognized.

"That library is really nice," I say carefully. "How old is it?"

"Almost a year." He doesn't seem to suspect what I'm really asking.

Then, just as the last of the town fades down the road, we pass a pool—excuse me, an *aquatics center*—and my control snaps.

In a town like this, somebody put up the money for all

this. Somebody important. Somebody who didn't put their name on all of it. And I have no idea why he wouldn't.

"Did you build all this?" I ask.

"With my own two hands? No."

Classic evasion. "Why don't you want anyone to know? Wait, do they even know how wealthy you are? Is that why you're driving a truck?"

His mouth flattens. Without his beard, I can see so much more of what he's feeling. "I'm driving the truck because the roads out here would tear the Tesla to shit."

I wait. He gives nothing else. "Come on. Stop holding back."

This game of his isn't so cute anymore, not when I'm falling for him and want to know what he's hiding. And why. He didn't bring me here by accident. He wanted me to see Ray, but he also wanted me to see this. To know this about him.

He sighs heavily. "Okay, I did give the money for all this. This town was dying, and I could save it. So I did."

I don't understand why he's not proud of that, because he clearly isn't. "Everyone here has to know about you. About your wealth. They have to know you donated the money for all this. So why keep it a secret?"

I've never seen him look so grim. "I got all this money because we got lucky."

That's not true, and he's too smart to actually believe that, but I leave it.

"All those guys I left behind," he says, "they're not any better or worse than I am. I'm not going to rub their noses in what I have and they don't. People get weird when you get rich, especially when you get rich like I did. I wanted this place to remain home and not get weird. Or die."

"You don't like talking about this." Which is a silly thing to say, because his entire body is pulled tighter than my braids in second grade.

"No."

No, he doesn't like talking about stuff that matters most to him. He wants to hide it, keep it safe. His life hasn't been easy, and his reluctance to crow about how far he's come—or to say anything at all—is heartwarming. And heart wrenching.

"I'd like to meet some of your friends," I say, keeping the emotional wobble out of my voice. "Hear about all the ridiculous stuff you did as a teenager."

"Why, so you can tease me about it?" But he's smiling and the tension is gone.

Maybe he wanted me to see this because he wanted to test me and my reaction to it. I think I passed.

"Exactly."

"They'll have a lot of stories." He turns off the highway onto the access road to the prison. "I've never brought a girl home before, and they'll be dying to spill."

I'm his girl. It's old-fashioned and kind of sexist, and I haven't been an actual girl since elementary school, but I like it. It's warm and cozy, and man, do I feel so incredibly special.

"I can't wait," I say. "Do they know we're coming?"

He shakes his head. "We can't this trip. We need to get into that data."

"But you stopped so I could see Ray?"

The prison is coming closer now, all looming and ugly and horrible.

"Yeah," he says, "but we can make time for that. And like I said, it's on the way."

Finn doesn't come inside with me. We're lucky that we arrived during visitation hours and that Ray wasn't in one of the psychiatric beds they keep for the seriously mentally ill prisoners. But Finn probably arranged all that too.

When Ray comes into the visiting room, he looks… tired. Puffy. Unfocused.

People have always told us how much we look alike, but we never saw it. Ray's forehead is broader than mine, his hair lighter, and his jaw is stronger. Our chins are the same, or same-ish—too prominent to be fashionable—but that's about it. Still, there's no face in the world I know better than my brother's.

"Ramona." His face cracks into the biggest smile. "You didn't tell me you were coming."

"It was kind of last minute. Hey, thanks for the notes you sent me on that issue with the AI. It really helped with the processing time."

His smile is faded. "It's nice to remember that I can think sometimes. Not like I used to, of course."

I force down the lump in my throat. "Of course you can still think." I take in the puffiness in his face, the unfocused gaze. "Are you back on your meds?"

His expression falls. "I figured I'd try again. There's a new one, I can't remember the name, but it's supposed to be better than the others."

The side effects don't look much better than the others, but if he can handle it and they cut down on his hallucinations, then great.

"Good," I say. "That's great if you're feeling better on them."

"How're my cats?"

Oh crap. I don't know what to tell him about Kevin. It will upset him, and there's nothing he can do from inside here, and I definitely do not want to trigger an episode.

But I also don't want to treat him like a child. He's ill, not incapacitated. And he did say the new meds were helping.

"You remember that construction site?" I ask. "The high-rise apartments they're putting in?"

His mouth twitches. "There were a few of them. We used to camp in one when it was really cold. But what about my cats?"

Oh no. Maybe Kevin did start that fire if he was sleeping in the building. "I'm getting to the cats," I say. "And don't worry, they're fine. Did you ever have fires when you camped there?"

"No. We're not stupid."

"Well, there was a fire, and the police arrested Kevin for it."

His face shifts, hardening into rage. "We didn't fucking do it! How many times do I have to say that?"

The guard looks over at us, and my heart jumps. "Ray, I know. I know. I'm only telling you what happened."

He shakes his head, still muttering. "Nobody believes me. I'm not crazy. I didn't imagine that. It was the camera, that camera wouldn't stop looking at me…"

A chill runs over me. "Wait, what camera?"

"I told you about it. The camera that wouldn't stop looking at me. I tried to hide from it, but it kept finding me."

He *had* told me about it. I remember now, but I thought it was a hallucination. "The camera took pictures of you? Where was it?"

"It followed me," he says slowly, frustrated. "It wasn't anywhere but behind me." He grabs his forehead. "Wait, that isn't right. I can't remember what's right."

My heart starts to sink. This isn't going to work, not the way I want it to. Anything my brother says might be real or might be a remembered hallucination. I won't be able to tell. And none of it would convince a judge to release him.

If Corvus was following my brother, if they did target him, they picked the perfect victim, the one nobody would ever believe.

"I know you're telling the truth about the camera," I say. "And I'm going to prove it."

Everyone will have to believe Corvus's own data.

"You found something?" he asks.

"I think so. But I don't know for sure yet."

He looks away, his mouth tight. "Thanks," he says roughly. "I know this hasn't been easy."

I take his hand. It's sunburned and rough. "Nothing I've faced has been even a hundredth as hard as what you've had to deal with. And I never, ever let myself forget that."

He makes himself smile. "Once I'm out of here, we'll program AIs together. I promise."

"Good. I can't wait to leave all the hard math to you." I give his hand one last squeeze. "I've got to go, but I promise I'm working on something big to get you out."

"A jailbreak?"

The guard looks sharply over at us. I guess jailbreak jokes aren't kosher here.

I suppress my laughter. "I'll just say if you get a cake, look for a file before you bite into it."

He lets go of my hand. "You'd better hurry up then. Because once I get that tunnel finished, I'm out." He smiles wistfully. "Thanks for coming. Oh, and what happened to my cats?"

I rise from the table. It's time to go. "I'm taking care of them. I never realized they were so picky—they'll only eat the fancy brand of food."

"Yeah, they're spoiled." He raps on the table once, then heads for the door. "Thanks for watching them."

We don't hug. Ray was never a hugger, and he got more shy about physical contact after his illness.

As I watch him go, I realize I never told him about Finn. I should have; I feel like they should know each other. But if we can get Ray out, there will be plenty of time for that.

Hang on, I promise my brother. *It won't be long now.*

I should have known stealing the data would be the easy part.

We're at my place in Baja, right on the beach, eating fish tacos and soaking up the sun. And trying to crack into the files I stole from Corvus.

Doc paces the office, chewing on her fingernail. "What did Grace say about the encryption again?"

We've been at this for only a few hours, but Doc's patience is already frayed. She's been keyed up ever since she visited her brother, which is understandable. She thinks this will get him out of prison.

I have my doubts, but she doesn't need to know that. When I came back from Corvus and said those things about doing something together in the future and she looked back at me like she did… I realized then I never wanted to disappoint this woman. I wanted to make her every dream reality.

So I took her to see her brother, just because I could. I'm not letting myself think too deeply about what I've done for her and what I want to do for her in the future though. We've got work to do, and I don't like to dwell on my feelings too much. Makes me all itchy inside.

"She said the data can only be read on a Corvus machine," I say. "They're probably running some kind of encryption app on each machine that encodes everything and decodes it when you call it up. That's why I could see the files in the server farm but can't see them here."

When we popped in the USB drive, expecting the secrets of Corvus to be open to us, we were disappointed. All the files were just gibberish.

Okay, so Fuchs isn't quite as dumb about security as I thought he was. This is definitely a big roadblock, but one I was anticipating.

Now I just have to crack this encryption. *We* have to crack this encryption—Doc knows as much about the subject as I do.

"So we need to write a similar program," she says, shaking out her hands as she paces.

"Or we could brute force it." And go swim in the ocean while the computer cranks away at that.

"We'd need a server…" Realization spreads over her face. "Right. You have a server farm here, don't you?"

"A modest one."

She bites her lip, which makes me want to bite her in the same spot. And then kiss it to soothe the ache. "We could, but that could take hours. Or days."

"Or weeks. We've got enough tequila to last us through the zombie apocalypse though, so we're safe on that front."

She shakes her head, the gesture amused. "You can't think of anything else?"

"I am thinking." I steeple my fingers, stare off at the ocean in the distance. "But I can't make inspiration strike. That's why I come here. I can enjoy myself while I wait for it."

She stops, staring at me. "Or maybe your inspiration is delayed because you're having too much fun."

Maybe. But I don't have to rush things anymore, so I don't. "Trust me, the solution will come. Probably when we're not even looking for it."

She's turned to the ocean, her gaze distant and wistful. The waves are calling to her too.

"We could take a swim," I say, "lie on the sand, have some cold beers. There's a double-sized hammock on the back porch—we could take a nap together."

Or try hammock sex. I've always been curious about that.

"Mmm." She taps her finger against her lips. "Maybe…"

"Not maybe. Let's do it."

"No." Her attention snaps back to me. "That's not what I meant. Do we still have the code Grace passed on to January, the stuff from Corvus's cell phone project?"

I immediately see where she's going. "I don't know if they encrypted the data they were pulling off people's phones though."

"But if they did, it might be the same encryption system." Her eyes are bright with anticipation.

"You are a genius." I'm already calling up the files on my desktop machine, so I can't see her expression.

"You're the genius." She's come up behind me, and her voice is a touch shaky.

I glance back at her. Goddamn but she's beautiful. "I didn't even consider that. And you did."

"Well, that ocean view is distracting."

I smack my hand on the desk in triumph. "There it is. And yep, they did encrypt that data."

She releases a deep exhale. "Oh, thank God."

It takes some tweaking before the encryption program is ready to run on my machine. Doc adds comments here and there, and soon enough, we've got it running.

"Ready?" I ask, my cursor hovering over the stolen files. If this doesn't work, we still have other options, but if it does, we can be inside this data in the next moment.

"Yes," Doc says, her mouth tense. She wants this to work even more than I do.

"Hold on to your butts." I click open the files.

The cursor switches to the Pinwheel of Death. Fuck. Maybe the machine is just having a cough as it opens the files.

We wait. Doc's hand comes to my shoulder. As the cursor keeps spinning, her grip gets tighter and tighter. Just like my gut is doing.

"Hang on," I say softly. "Just give it a minute."

The seconds keep ticking away. This bullshit machine won't even fucking open some files… If this piece of shit crashes, I'm going to punch the tower. I don't care if I do break something.

Her nails are digging into my shirt. I put a hand over hers. Of course I'm not going to punch anything. I've got to stay chill for her.

She sighs. "It's not going to—"

A dozen files pop up, then a dozen more. And more and more until over a hundred file folders fill the window.

Her hand flutters under mine. "It worked." She sounds like she can't believe it.

"Maybe. Let's take a look under the hood."

I click on one of the folders labeled Client Specs. Several document files appear. When I open one, it's all there in plain English.

"Homeless crime statistics," Doc reads off. "And sentencing averages."

"What the hell?" I quickly scroll through the document. It's a compilation of crimes that homeless people have been arrested for in the past year, their conviction rates, and how long their sentences were.

The last sentence utterly chills me: "We determine then that crimes of arson, aggravated robbery, and assault are most likely to garner convictions with the longest prison sentences. We therefore suggest targeting identified, unwanted homeless with these crimes in order to remove them from society for the most amount of time."

"Remove them from society?" Doc rubs her hand over her face. "They're teaming up with the Oakland PD to remove homeless people from the streets and warehouse them in the prison system. I guess busing them somewhere else just wasn't enough."

I reach for my beard, then remember I don't have it anymore. "But they don't need Corvus for that. Just somebody decent at programming in R." I hold up my palm. "Let's go through the rest of it before we come to any conclusions."

Her expression is mutinous, but she doesn't say anything. I mean, I agree that the document is pretty damning, but we've got over a hundred more of these things to go through.

The next few files are all pictures and videos, mostly of homeless people in various neighborhoods in Oakland. When Ray comes on the screen, Doc gasps.

"See?" She stabs at the screen. "It was them. They set him up."

This doesn't really prove that. At least not in the legal sense. "They were tracking him," I say. "But we already knew that."

I quickly click over to another folder. This one's filled with the tracking data from the videos. There are a series of numbers—I'm guessing they gave each person they were tracking a number—and all the statistics of their routes through the day.

Okay, Oakland PD would probably need Corvus for this.

At the end of each record is a notation—robbery, assault, or arson—and a location. I frown as I try to puzzle out what that means.

Doc's already ahead of me though. She grabs the mouse and starts frantically scrolling through the document. "There." She points to one record. "Robbery. CVS at the corner of 41st and Howe. That's Ray. They calculated what they could most likely convict him of and where and then pinned it on him."

"But that's just a number. We have no way to connect it to Ray."

She flings up her hands. "Then cross-reference it with the labels from the videos!"

She's getting worked up, which is understandable—it's her brother after all—but that's no way to work through this data. She's only going to be looking for what she wants rather than what's really there.

"I'm going to do that," I say. "But let's finish going through this."

A lot of the rest is code for their AI, the tracking program, the facial recognition. There's a bunch of testing protocols and data. Nothing too interesting, although I'll pull apart their algorithm later.

Doc starts to pace again. I bring a chair over next to mine. "Sit. I can't think when you do that."

"What do you need to think for?" she mutters. But she sits.

I start to go methodically through each file, taking notes in my head. So far, this all looks bad, but it's not *bad* bad. I mean, cops have been targeting homeless people forever. Now they're just bringing computers into it.

I come across a document titled Client Prospectus. When I see the client name, my brain stops.

"That's not right," I say. That's not the client. The client is supposed to be the Oakland PD.

Doc is rising out of her chair, leaning close to the computer screen. "That's the construction company."

"What construction company?"

"The one that's building all the high-rises in my neighborhood. Gordian Development. The one that owns the site where Kevin supposedly started that fire."

I keep reading through the document. "So Corvus is targeting homeless people for a developer? And not the Oakland PD?"

"We promise to deliver to the Oakland PD identified undesirables in the defined neighborhoods," Doc reads. "We aim for an eighty percent conviction rate of the undesirables with an average sentence of five years. We predict a fifty-three percent rise in property values after a three-month implementation of the Oracular program."

I sit back hard in my chair. "Motherfucker. *Motherfucker.*"

Corvus is being paid by this Gordian Development group to identify *undesirables*—read, anybody that doesn't fit into their newly gentrified neighborhoods—and pass that info on to the Oakland PD so said undesirables can be convicted and carted off to prison.

And then all the property Gordian owns goes up in value. It's gentrification on steroids.

"Look." Doc scrolls through to the document to a section titled Test Case. "Oh my God. Ray was their test case."

Sure enough, they describe how they tracked her brother, calculated the most likely place he'd commit a crime, and what crime he'd most likely be convicted of. They even had the faked pictures they'd used at his trial.

"'Mr. Blythe is a paranoid schizophrenic, making his testimony unreliable in court.'" Doc is silently crying now, tears slipping down her cheeks. "They took advantage of him. They knew he wouldn't be believed. They were counting on it."

I take a tissue from the box on my desk and wipe her cheeks. "It's okay," I say. "It'll be okay."

I'll make it okay somehow. Her tears are tearing my heart into a thousand tiny, bleeding pieces. I don't know what a lawyer will make of this, but she was right all along. Her brother was framed.

"We'll take all this to a lawyer," I say. "We'll find the best one, hell, a whole team of them, and give them this. They'll figure something out. Ray will get out."

I have no idea how they'll use it though; it's all inadmissible because I stole it. Fuck. I'll have to get Ray out of prison some other way. A quieter way.

She wipes her eyes. "But I've already gone to lawyers. I've spent a fortune on them. I need something bigger. More public."

The hair on the back of my neck rises. Public? I don't do public. It's one thing to have rumors of my hacking into places I shouldn't—it's another to have it confirmed. "What do you mean?"

"I mean…" She stares at the screen, her brow creasing. "What's happening?"

The cursor has gone back to a pinwheel even though nothing should be loading.

"The fuck?" I try to call up a command window, but nothing happens. It's just frozen. "Goddammit, what's going on?"

The screen goes black. And stays that way.

Nothing gets the machine to come back even though I smash the keyboard hard enough to crack one of the keys. The screen remains dead. I have to do a hard restart.

Only, it doesn't restart. It gets to the start-up screen, then tells me it can't find a hard drive.

Punching a tower never works, but I want to do it so badly right now.

"It's dead," Doc says. Her voice is hollow. "All that work, all that evidence… and it's gone."

I start to say that maybe the USB drive is okay, but I know it's not. This was a dead man's switch, a hidden trigger that somehow sensed something was off and then erased everything.

I put my head in my hands. Fuck. Fuck. I've got a copy of the data, but it's going to do the same damn thing to any other machine it's put on. And I don't know if I can find the switch in time to keep it from melting another machine.

There's nothing to take to a lawyer except Doc's suspicions. And she's already done that.

We're back to square one, except we know how far we could have gone now.

Worst of all is that I've disappointed her. I promised her something good would come from this break-in, and I've failed her.

"We can't get it back, can we?" Doc's words are so quiet I barely hear them.

"We will." I lift my head. "It's just going to take more time." I can fix this. I can always fix things.

"That's what the lawyers said. Always more time. While Ray is stuck there."

The defeat in her voice kills me. "Hey, this is fixable. Let's go for a swim, take a break, come back to it later."

"And destroy another machine?" She shakes her head. "I need to go lie down. I was so close this time… And…" Her shoulders begin to shake. "I'm sorry. I just need to be alone."

Before I can stop her, she's gone.

Somehow the beauty outside the bedroom window makes my grief that much darker. Like the entire world has decided to go on being bright and gorgeous as a personal eff you to me.

I picked one of the guest bedrooms to hide in. It's all very slick and modern, the bed done up in grays, the walls a subtle echo of that same color, and a teak hardwood floor, with french doors that open up onto the beach. It's so perfect as to be a dream.

Curled on the bed, watching the waves roll in and letting the tears slip down my cheeks, it feels more like a nightmare.

I could have saved Ray. Everything was there, everything I somehow knew in my gut was always true. He was innocent, and he was targeted because some developer thought he was "undesirable."

I bet they've done the same thing to Kevin. And they'll do the same to everyone else they think doesn't deserve to live in their new, shiny Oakland.

God, this is the worst thing in the world to know what Corvus and Gordian are up to, to know they're ruining lives but to be completely helpless to stop them. Yeah, we can get the data back, probably, but how much longer will that take?

I want justice *now*.

I roll over on the bed, blocking out the view of the ocean. This wall has what looks like an expressionist oil painting on it, although I don't recognize the artist. It's a woman's face, done in white and deep orange and acid yellows and poison blues. Her features melt into the paint strokes, which drag across the canvas. She looks like she's dissolving into streaks of color.

I can sympathize.

This is silly. I should go find Finn, let him make me feel better. He will.

Except, when he was talking about swimming and the beach, it felt… wrong. Like I'd be betraying Ray if I did anything but try to recover that data. I know he was only trying to help me, but I don't want to feel better. I want to be angry. Everything that's happened to my brother is just so messed up.

What I really want to do is talk to January. I shouldn't have listened to Finn's nonsense about keeping all this quiet. She might even be able to help us.

I roll over and reach for my phone on the bedside table. Huh. My secure messaging app has a notification. Looks like January already tried to reach me.

When I open it, it's not from January. The sender's name is only a string of numbers, and the message says: *You tripped the dead man's switch. This should help.*

Some files are attached. I don't know if I should open them. What if they wipe my phone?

But this is my secure app. The only way to message me through this is to get the program from January. Fuchs once messaged January through it, but that was because he stole Grace's phone.

Which means… I'm not exactly sure what it means. Someone inside Corvus knows we have this data and that we set off their trap. But instead of accusing us of theft, they're claiming to want to help us.

I grab my phone and go to find Finn.

He's still in his office, staring off at the view. Without his beard, he looks younger. More vulnerable.

He risked a lot to get this data. And when it disappeared, he must have felt as devastated as I did.

"Hey."

When he turns and sees me, he smiles, but I can see the effort behind it. "Are you feeling better?"

"Not really." I hold up my phone. "Something very weird just came through on the secure messaging app."

I set the phone on the desk in front of him. He reads through the message quickly, frowning when he gets to the end. "What the hell?"

"It has to be someone from Corvus. But how would they access the app? And are those files just a trap?"

He's chewing on the side of his lip, and even though I'm worked up, I can't help but notice how cute it is. "The dead man's switch is already triggered, and they know it. Why send another file?"

"Why would anyone from Corvus help us at all?"

"Grace did." He sets the phone down. "Let's open this on your laptop."

His confidence is catching. But still, I hold back. "And if it fries my laptop?"

"I'll buy you a new one. Come on, aren't you curious?" The swagger and bravado is thick in his voice, just like when he was daring me to play him at Go.

I am curious, desperately so. But I've also been burned before.

"Fine." I grab my laptop from my bag and fire up the messaging app. But once the mysterious message is up, I can't make myself open the files.

Finn reaches over me, his arm brushing my shoulder, his scent filling my nose. "See?" He double clicks and the download window pops up. "Easy enough."

We both frown at the screen. It looks like the same files we got from Corvus before, only completely unencrypted. There's even some extra there—an email chain between the COO of Gordian and the lead on the Corvus project, detailing timelines, implementation, and integration with the Oakland PD's panopticon.

I can hardly breathe. This is even more explosive than what we had before. And someone just gave it to us.

"Who is this person?" I whisper.

"I have no idea." Finn sounds as baffled as I am. "What the fuck is going on?"

I can't answer that. It's like seeing a miracle. I wished so long and hard for something, anything, to happen to help Ray, and here it is. I want to believe, so badly, and at the same time I don't. If it's not real…

"Should we check for another dead man's switch?" I ask.

Finn starts methodically opening all the files, poking around in the code. Every time he does, I hold my breath, waiting for the screen to go black.

It never comes.

Finally he gets to the last file. It sits open for a minute, then two, then three. Still my laptop hums away.

And finally I let myself *believe*. And act.

"We have to call Callie right now," I say. "How soon can she publish this?"

Finn sits back, crosses his arms. He looks… grim. "We're not publishing it."

That… that's not computing. I cock my head, replay his words. That's not what he said. It couldn't be. He wouldn't just hide this away. It's way too explosive. Innocent lives have been ruined because of it. There needs to be justice.

"I don't understand," I say slowly. "We're taking this public, right?"

I wait for him to tell me that I've misunderstood, that I've got it all wrong.

He doesn't. Instead, his expression goes even grimmer. "That's exactly what I mean. We take it to a lawyer, see what he can do for your brother. And then I'm going to tell Fuchs I have this."

"You're going to tell Fuchs?" Cold realization spreads through my veins. "You're going to use this to bargain with him?"

That's only half a question.

It suddenly occurs to me that this man isn't just Finn, the funny daredevil who happens to be an amazing hacker, great in bed, and really good at Go. He's also a partner in one of the biggest venture capital firms in the Valley. He might be Fuchs's natural enemy, but in many ways they're more alike than they are different.

Finn's never even met my brother. It's not that he doesn't care—he's willing to give all this to a team of lawyers he'll pay for—but what he and I care about are two very different things.

"Not bargaining," he says. "But I don't want the whole world to know I hacked Corvus and neither does Fuchs. I'll use this to make sure the program goes away. Quietly. Plus I'll dangle the bait of the mole in his organization. He won't be able to resist that."

"It doesn't just need to be shut down." I'm close to shouting. "It also needs to be exposed. People have a right to know. And you're going to sell out the person who helped us?"

Finn snorts, like I've just said the most naive thing ever. "Who is this person? You don't know and neither do I. I'm not selling anyone out personally. As for 'right to know,' nobody has a right to know anything. What, is it written in the Constitution that everybody's entitled to know about surveillance programs? This isn't the first of its kind, and it won't be the last. Nobody really cared when they found out

Facebook, Google, and everything else was selling their information. So why would they care about this?"

"Because..." *Because it was my brother who was hurt.* But really, I'm the only one who cares. Everyone else might agree with Corvus—he's undesirable. "Because the only way to know if people will care is to tell them about it."

But he's ready for that. "Some of the stuff we did was illegal. Which is why hackers don't brag openly about their shit. Are you really willing to go to jail to expose this?"

I lift my chin. "Of course I am. Remember, my brother is already there because of this horrible program."

Finn closes his eyes as if he's in pain. "This... You have to understand. If we can destroy this thing from the shadows, it's still destroyed."

"And you get to keep playing your hacker games without anyone else knowing." I close my own eyes now, because we just keep going past each other. And I don't think we'll ever meet again. "This is all just pieces on a Go board to you, isn't it?"

God forbid anything interfere with his *games.* Or that anyone see him as something beyond the hacker, the redneck, the joker.

That pisses him off. "Exposing this program and revealing our role in uncovering it isn't gonna do a damn thing except make you feel like a martyr. Like your protest— you could shout and yell and feel like you did something, but in the end the police are going to win."

My mouth falls open as my heart breaks. He doesn't want to expose the program, but he also doesn't want to expose *himself.* Not even for me. "That's the most cynical thing I've ever heard."

"What, you thought I was just a clown? You don't break in the systems I have by being a jerk-off all the time. Sorry, I don't go in for the symbolic gesture. I prefer the ones that actually work."

He's being deliberately cruel now, and I feel every word like blows. "No, I get it now. You've made it very clear." I cross my arms over my chest, trying to hold in everything. "Could you please call the jet? I want to go home."

I don't know what I'll do when I get there, but I'm definitely telling January about all this. No more secrets.

Finn stares at me for a long moment. I don't want to parse what's running through his expression, so I don't. "Fine. If that's how you feel."

"It is. And just so you know, I'm going to make all this public. That person from Corvus sent that data to me, not you. They took a risk to expose this. I'm going to honor that."

"You do whatever makes you happy." He grabs his phone. "You'd better start packing."

I want to stop this, to turn everything around and start over. To beg him not to let it end like this.

But it's too late for that. He chose his path, and I chose mine.

CHAPTER 25

I really fucked that up.

I know it the moment Doc walks out of the house, but because I'm a stupid bastard, it takes me a little longer to really *know* it.

Fuck, I'm going to have to grovel here. Like epic, develop calluses on my knees, beg and plead and promise anything, grovel.

You're right. That's what I'll lead off with, because it's true. They railroaded her brother. The man deserves to have his name cleared publicly.

We'll go to the press. That one's a little harder to imagine myself saying. We could leak it anonymously, but that won't have as much impact. And it might not lead to Corvus shutting it down.

Everyone's going to know, absolutely, positively, not even a rumor anymore that I'm hacking into other people's companies. Maybe even *their* companies. My social and business life is going to suck for a while. And having everyone know... My skin itches like crazy at the thought. Hell, my insides are even itching.

Doc's not going to want to hear that though. She wants

justice, and she wants the whole world to know about it. I suppose she deserves that.

I have to make it happen for her then.

I glance at the clock. She's just now arriving at the airstrip. The jet will be fueled and waiting for her, ready to take her wherever she wants to go. She left without even saying goodbye.

Fuck, I hope I can grovel well enough to get her back. If I can't…

The thought leaves me even colder than imagining my hacking activities exposed to everyone. I think… I think I might need her. Need her more than anything.

Oh fuck it—I know I need her. Like more than I need my next breath.

I shove my chair away from the desk as the realization sits on my chest, heavy and big as an elephant.

I fucking love her. Like, with all my heart.

I love playing Go with her, even when she sets an AI on me. I love hanging out with her in tiny jazz bars. Or in massive penthouses.

I love how quick she is, how sarcastic she is, how smart she is. And I love how idealistic she is even if it massively fucks things up for me.

I want to enjoy every bit of her for the rest of my life. Love every bit of her for the rest of my life.

And I was a supreme asshole to her. I put my head in my hands. I am such an idiot.

I've got to get to the airstrip. There's just enough time to catch her, to tell her everything. I reach for my keys on the desk—and I see something that catches my attention.

The files that mole sent us are still open on her laptop. She left that behind in her rush to leave me. There, sitting among the documents and videos and data, is something I missed the first time through.

I open it, scrolling through the code. How the hell did that slip past *me*?

It's a key to Corvus's back door. The holy grail of cracking into that place. And whoever this person is just stuck it in there.

Which means… they want us to have access.

I lift my hands from the keyboard. This… this could solve everything.

I scramble for my phone, punch in the number for the airstrip.

"Hello, Mr. Braden. The jet's ready, just as you requested, and the lady has already boarded."

"Don't let that jet leave. Keep it on the runway. I need to be on it when it leaves." I snap shut Doc's laptop, grab whatever else I think I'll need.

"Of course, sir, it's just… Ms. Blythe seems very irritated. She keeps asking when we're leaving. Quite forcefully."

"Yeah." I grab my other cell phone, start dialing another number. The sooner I can get to that plane, the better, but I need to set some stuff in motion first. "We had a little bit of a fight. Now I need to get out there and tell her she was right all along."

The man laughs. "Good luck. Looking at her expression, I'd say it would have to be a pretty extravagant apology."

"I've got something good in mind."

The other phone in my hand rings, then I hear a faint "Hello?"

"I've gotta go," I tell the cabin manager. "Keep that plane there."

I put the other phone to my ear. "Dev?"

"Finn. What's up?"

He doesn't sound surprised to hear from me, but Dev is never surprised by anything.

"I've got a back door into Corvus—"

"Wait." He's not surprised, just skeptical. "No, you don't."

"Well, I haven't opened it yet to see if it's real, but I'm pretty sure it is." I drum my fingers on the desk. As much as I love bantering with Dev, I need to get to that airstrip. Every minute I'm here is another minute for Doc to think up reasons why we shouldn't be together.

"Does this have to do with your trip to Corvus last week?"

I sit up. "How did you know about that?"

"There have been rumors about Fuchs losing his shit over a breach. Nothing concrete, but the head of Corvus security has resigned."

"Yeah, he got fired." It looks like Fuchs found out about our break-in and lopped off some heads.

"So you did sneak into the building?"

My initial instinct is to deny, deny, deny. If Dev were Elliot, our lawyer, that's definitely what I'd do. Elliot doesn't need to know about the illegal shit I do—he needs plausible deniability.

Dev though… He could know. He'd never rat me out.

But still, he doesn't need to know.

I sigh. If I'm going to win Doc back, I need to turn over a new, more open leaf. Starting now. "Yeah, as a plumber. Doc helped me."

"Doc?"

"January's Doc. I'm in love with her."

Now that, that was easy to say. Felt really good too. Huh. I probably should have said it sooner, preferably to Doc first.

"What?" Oh boy, Dev is definitely surprised now. I didn't think he had it in him. "When did this happen?"

"It's been happening. She's pissed at me, but I'm going to win her back. Which I need your help with."

"My help?"

My other phone starts to ring. Shit, it's the airstrip. I really hope Doc hasn't commandeered the plane and is flying herself back to Oakland.

"I need a virus," I say quickly. "A really nasty one, and quick. I don't have time to code one myself."

Dev is closemouthed about it, but he has a ton of black hat connections. He'll be able to find what I need and fast.

There's a long beat of silence. "Are you sure about that?"

"Don't tell me you're afraid of Corvus. It'll be targeted, I promise." Which reminds me, we'll need Grace's help for this.

"Fine. Am I allowed to tell everyone else you're in love?"

"Sure. It's not a secret."

I can almost hear Dev shaking his head. "I don't like all the romance going on around here. First Mark, then Logan, now you… It's… it's bad for business. You guys need to be focused here, on the office."

I very carefully and most definitely do not mention whatever is going on with him and Anjie. "There's still you and Paul and Elliot. Paul will never get married—he'd never hear the end of it from his mom, and Elliot will never find someone as anal retentive as he is. And you… You're the man of mystery. Getting married would ruin all that. So the rest of you are completely safe."

Dev doesn't reply to that. "I'll get your virus. When will you be back?"

I check the time again. Fifteen minutes to the airstrip, maybe half an hour to convince Doc—better make it a full hour—then the flight back… "We'll be in the office by eight. Or wait, meet us at the secure facility. And get Grace there too."

Dev sighs heavily. "Anything else? Caviar? Champagne waiting?"

"That's a great idea, because we'll have a lot of celebrating to do if this works. Except we're not champagne people. Stop by that place in Lower Haight, get us some bottles of the triple, and pick up some sausages from the grill next door."

"I never should've answered the phone," Dev mutters.

"But you did. I gotta go. See you soon."

"I wish I weren't." Dev's tone is grudging, but I can hear the love.

Speaking of love… "I'm out. And… thanks."

Dev doesn't get choked up. "Just go fix whatever you did with Doc. You're going to be useless around here until you do."

I hang up and rush out to do just that.

CHAPTER 26

This plane can't leave fast enough.

Not because I'm that eager to leave Finn behind but because I'm worried if we stay here too much longer, I'll bolt off the plane and demand to be taken back to him.

That fight didn't end the way it should have. The more that I think about it, he might be right. Not about everything but about just running to the press. Fuchs is known to be a vindictive ass; if I openly admit I stole from him, he'll grind me into dust. And maybe even Finn too, although that would be a lot harder to do.

Exposing the truth isn't going to get Ray released right away. I've been banging my head against the justice system for years now—the warden isn't going to read about the Oracular project and let Ray go in the next minute. There would have to be hearings, procedures, paperwork… more lawyers to hire.

Always more lawyers to hire.

But keeping it quiet and using it as private leverage against Fuchs? That's not right. He needs to hurt. And we need to destroy the Oracular program.

The problem is I don't know that exposing the program

will be enough to stop it. Finn had some good points about how people don't care.

Maybe… maybe I should get off the plane. We can talk it over again, more calmly. We were both worked up after everything that happened.

But the crew is all on board, the captain is sealed in the cockpit, and the engines are humming. I can't imagine how much it is to get a jet like this ready to fly. It's probably nothing to Finn, but I still feel guilty when I think about the expense, which would be wasted if I got off.

Yeah, it's better that I stay on the plane. We can meet in the City once we've both cooled off. That would be best.

Except… Tears spring to my eyes. I don't want to leave like this. I don't want to leave at all. I want to be with him tonight, tomorrow morning, tomorrow evening, basically all the time.

I want him. Totally and completely. Because I love him. I love his genius brain, his quick and dirty wit, his amazing body, and the way he smiles. And the way he makes me smile.

Crap. That does it. I fumble with the seat belt. "Excuse me?" I call up to the crew. "Excuse me, but I need to get off this plane."

"What?" The nice man who gave me a glass of champagne when I came on board pops his head out of the galley. "No, miss, you can't do that."

I push up out of the chair. "I'm so sorry, but I have to. Could you please call the car back?"

"I'm not supposed to—" He swallows hard when he catches my expression. "One moment." He picks up the phone, calling someone while he watches me. After a few seconds, he sets the phone down. "I'm sorry, miss, but the driver isn't answering. Could you wait a little longer while I try to contact him? We have more champagne."

I consider that. I don't have to do the driving, and it was

very nice champagne. "Okay. But could you please hurry? I really do need to go."

Fifteen minutes and two glasses later, I'm starting to suspect something is up. "Did you get ahold of the driver?" I ask for what feels like the twentieth time. "I don't want to be a bother, but I have to go. It's important."

The steward hesitates. "Just a little while longer."

He's lying to me. I'm not sure how I know, but he is. "Okay, I'm getting off now. Car or no."

"Miss, no—"

I shove past him, aiming for the open hatch and the stair car. I doubt he'd physically restrain me, but I'm determined to get out of here. I've had enough.

I shoot through the open hatch, slipping right past the steward, ready to dash down the stairs.

And I smash straight into Finn.

He catches me as easily as if I were a pillow. "Jesus. You could break your neck."

"Oh." I push the hair out of my face. "It's you."

I'm so surprised to see him I can't think of anything better to say. And his closeness, his arms curving protectively around me, is scrambling my thoughts.

"Yeah." His expression is startled. "I've got some stuff to tell you. A lot of stuff."

I can't tell if it's good stuff or bad stuff. Whichever it is, I have to hear him out. I point to the plane behind us. "They have champagne. If you want some while you tell me stuff."

Within a few minutes, we're arranged in the cabin, tucked into the plush leather chairs and each gripping a flute of champagne. I resolve to go slow with mine since this is number four for me. I'm also not exactly emotionally stable at the moment, what with falling for him and fighting with him and trying to figure out how to tell him all that.

"So." I take a small sip, my hands shaking. "You wanted to talk."

Finn sighs heavily. "I have to tell you… I was wrong. Completely and totally wrong and I'm sorry."

"Oh." Out of everything I was expecting him to say, that wasn't it. "Wrong about what?"

"All of it." His hand is gripping the flute stem way too tightly. He's going to snap it in two. "I never should have said those things to you. It's your brother—he deserves justice. And Oracular has to be stopped, permanently."

I rub my hand down the leather of the armrest. I can simply say I accept his apology and then we… do something from here, but I can't.

"I have to tell you some stuff too," I say. "I… I overreacted. You had a lot of good points, and I refused to listen. I wanted everything to happen immediately. But it doesn't work like that. I'm sorry if I hurt you."

He's suddenly on his knees before me, taking my hands. "We can't both be wrong. I made you cry. You're right—I'm a complete asshole. You don't have to forgive me."

His hands are so big and warm. I want to brush my cheeks over them. "I don't remember calling you a complete asshole. And we both handled this badly. Which… emotions were running high." I blink away some more tears, not sad ones. "We both feel deeply."

His expression opens with something like hope. "Yeah," he says slowly. "We do."

"Okay, we both admit we were jackasses." I smile down at him. I want to tell him how I feel, how much I love him, but this moment doesn't feel right. I've forgiven him, but we're not finished.

Still, I have to kiss him. His mouth tastes like cool champagne and warm man. His tongue brushes mine, and I shudder. This feels so good I can do it forever. We'll just live on this plane, parked on this runway, and the steward will bring us champagne every so often to keep our strength up.

Finn pulls away first, his expression wondering again, like

he can't believe how amazing this is. I probably look the same way.

"So what do we do now?" I ask.

He becomes Serious Finn. "We're going to get Ray out. And bring down Oracular. And we're going to do it both our ways."

It sounds great, and I wish it could happen, but... "How can we possibly do both our ways?"

"We'll release the data. But anonymously. I know it won't be as powerful as if we put our names on it, but I'll make sure it gets traction."

It makes sense, and it's more discreet than shouting it from the rooftops. I mean, I can still yell about how my brother is innocent and he was right all along—I just won't be able to say I was responsible for finding that out. Which is a small price to pay.

"Okay." I release a breath, letting go of that dream. "And Ray?"

"Once this comes out, we should be able to get him a new trial." His hands tighten on mine. "I can't guarantee anything, and I so wish I could, but this is probably the best chance he'll get. And I'll hire the lawyers that will make sure that chance is really fucking good."

My throat is tight. This is more hope—real hope—than Ray has had in a long time. "That's great." I blink hard. "Seriously, it's awesome. And if we can't take down Oracular, at least people will know about it."

I have to temper my expectations. I can't get everything I want. This is still a massive victory.

"Oh, we're taking down Oracular," he says. "From the inside."

I narrow my eyes. I don't like the idea of *inside* Corvus. Once in that place—twice, actually—was more than enough for me. And there's no way a disguise would work a second time. "What do you mean, from the inside?"

He's so excited he actually bounces. "A virus." He waggles his eyebrows. "A nasty one that will scramble everything related to Oracular. And it will get into the backup system too."

Wow. That sounds… delicious. Exactly the kind of revenge I want. "But won't Fuchs be furious?"

"Yeah, but he won't want to admit publicly that hackers got into his precious secure facility and fucked one of his programs. It would make him look bad to clients."

Finn's assurance is a dangerous thing. It makes me want to go along with this without any questions. But I've got some anyway. "Once the program's gone, what's he going to tell the police? Or Gordian?"

Finn shrugs. "That's his problem. We just need to make sure we can't be traced to the leak. Or the break-in. Not even a little bit."

I wiggle my fingers under his, thinking. "That means Callie can't publish it. She's way too close. Do you know anyone at *Disrupt Dispatch*?"

He smiles, slow and wicked. God, I love that smile. "Honey, I know everybody there. I've even got the personal email address of the editor in chief."

"Well then. I'm sure you know how to send it to them and cover your tracks."

"If there's one thing I'm good at, it's covering my tracks."

The hacker extraordinaire has returned, all cocky confidence. I can feel myself getting excited about this, ready to put the plan into motion and see what happens.

But we're forgetting one key detail. "How are we going to deliver this virus?" I ask. "I can't sneak into the building again."

His expression goes stony. "There's no fucking way I'm putting you in danger like that again. I was terrified the entire time."

I pull my hand free of his and set it against his cheek. He's letting his beard grow back, and there's almost a half inch of stubble there, surprisingly soft. In a few months, he'll look exactly the same again.

"That's funny," I say, "because I was terrified the entire time *you* were in there."

We smile together, and I can feel it, this thing between us we're not quite ready to name to each other. But it's there.

We can name it in our own good time. It's enough that it's there.

"We're not going back," he says. "Your friend inside Corvus gave us a key to the back door. We missed it the first time."

My mouth opens into a perfect O. "We have to meet this person someday. They're a freaking hero."

"Here's to hoping they reveal themselves."

The steward pokes his head in. He doesn't even bat an eye at Finn kneeling on the floor. "Refills?"

Finn doesn't get up, as if it's perfectly natural for him to be holding my hands and kneeling before me. Oh, and to have my hand on his cheek. "Yeah, one more. And then we should be off."

"Ah. Should I tell the pilot we're ready to depart then?"

Man, that steward would have been a perfect Edwardian butler. He's unflappable. We've kept this plane waiting for hours now.

"Yep." Finn's gaze locks with mine. "We're ready to go home."

CHAPTER 27

I figured Finn arranged everything beforehand like he always does, but I didn't expect him to arrange this much.

We go immediately to the secure facility from SFO, stopping by In-N-Out for some burgers.

"We'll need fuel," Finn says. "It could take all night."

I'm actually excited by that idea. Especially since I'll be spending the time with him.

When we arrive, Grace is there, already waiting for us. Along with—

"*Paul?*" Finn asks. "What are you doing here?"

"Why are you involving Grace with Corvus again?" Paul asks. "She doesn't need this. They're already targeting her."

Paul is as contained as ever, but there's no question he's pissed.

Grace shakes her head. "I told him it was fine. But he insisted on coming."

Finn and I share a look. There's only one explanation for Paul knowing that Grace was coming here on such short notice and going with her—they were together. But it's past office hours and they don't even work together.

"This isn't going to affect her immigration status," Finn

says. "I promise. We just need her help getting a key into a door."

Grace sits down firmly at a workstation. "I'm ready. I'll do anything I can to help."

Paul stands behind her. I'd call it hovering, but he's not the hovering type. It's more of a very, very classy glower.

"Nothing illegal," I say. "We just need you to explain some things, and then you can go." I definitely do not want to get Grace into any more trouble. Corvus is already messing with her visa stuff.

"Like I said, anything I can do to help." Grace sends Paul a look. "I'm not afraid."

Paul's mouth tightens, but that's it. He reaches into his jacket pocket and hands Finn a USB drive. "Dev sent this. He said to be careful with it."

That must be our virus. My heart picks up speed. This is really going to happen. We're going to strike a blow right at Corvus.

"Thanks." Finn takes it with a smile. He's not put off by Paul's irritation. "Doc, could you bring up the key for Grace to look at? I'm going to set up an anonymous email."

While he does that, Grace and I go through the key the mystery person sent us. Grace offers very vague advice, never mentioning anything too specific, never mentioning Corvus or Oracular by name. She's a canny one.

Paul stands over us, not saying anything, but he clearly disapproves. Grace doesn't seem to care, even though she's being remarkably careful. And opaque.

But she gives me more than enough. By the time Finn comes back over, my fingers are twitching because this might just work. And I can't wait to see if it will.

"I think we have everything," I say to him. When our eyes meet, sparks fly. We're both more than eager to do this. Man, this adrenaline high could get really addictive. Especially when I share it with him.

"Good. Paul, Grace, it might be time for you to go." Finn doesn't want them to see what we're doing—plausible deniability. I never thought about it before, but his secrecy when it comes to his hacking protects his friends as much as it does him.

I'm in the golden circle though. Which is the only place I want to be.

Paul uncrosses his arms, his mouth pursing. "All right," he says reluctantly. "I hope this works. I just… I just didn't want Grace in any more danger."

Grace looks up at him in surprise and shock. But Paul doesn't see it.

"She won't be." Finn claps him on the shoulder. "But I understand where you're coming from."

As Grace rises from her chair, she gives me two big thumbs-up. "You've got this. Whoever sent that to you knows what they're doing. They want you to get inside."

"You really have no idea who it is?" I ask.

Grace shakes her head regretfully. "I wish I did. Everything is so secret there, so compartmentalized… Even if someone did believe what Corvus is doing is wrong, there's no way to tell anyone else how you feel. It was the most isolating experience of my life."

This person who's reaching out to us probably feels the same way. I suddenly want this to work for more than just me or Finn or Ray—I want this virus to work for Grace and our mole and everyone else who's been hurt by Corvus. Even their employees.

"We'll get them," I promise. "We can't take the entire place down, but we can at least stop this."

Grace gives me a quick hug. "Once you're done, let's get drinks with January. I think we all have a lot to talk about."

"That sounds awesome."

She and Paul leave with a wave. And then it's just Finn

and me. He looks... big. Determined. Ready to fuck some shit up.

It's so sexy I want to jump him. After. We'll do that after.

I swallow and force myself to focus. "It should be pretty easy. We need to send it in small packets though so the security systems aren't triggered by a large upload."

"Great. I've sent all the files off to the editor of *Disrupt Dispatch*. He'll never suspect it was us—I made it sound like I was a Corvus employee leaking it, which isn't far from the truth. But that'll grab his attention and keep Fuchs off our scent." He sits in Grace's chair, his knee brushing mine. "Sending the virus in small packets is easy enough. But it'll take a while."

"We've got fuel," I remind him, pointing to the In-N-Out bags.

"And I've got just the thing to entertain us."

But he doesn't say what it is. Instead, he starts slowly, methodically working his way into the system as I guide him, using the advice Grace gave us. There're a million different ways we can trigger the security, so after every step we have to check and double-check that everything's still going smoothly.

It's nerve-racking, and sweat is gathering between my breasts, but it's also exhilarating. Finn is focused, confident, and watching him work is... It's hot.

"Okay." He takes a deep breath, pushes back from the desk. "We're in. The system thinks we're some VIP's VPN. We need to make it look like we're checking emails or messages."

He's set it up so it appears we're a bigwig remotely accessing the company's servers from home. To access the Corvus network, most people have to actually be at Corvus —that helps with security—but a few very important people are allowed full access from remote computers through a VPN.

"Can the system tell which VIP it thinks you are?" I ask.

He shakes his head. "There's nothing identifying here." He moves back to the keyboard. "Are you ready?"

My pulse kicks against my skin. Suddenly I'm not sure if I am. What we're doing is so risky. I could end up in a jail cell right next to my brother's.

But it's also high reward. And I'm feeling lucky for the first time in forever.

I nod. "Let's do it."

Finn hits a few keys and starts the upload. It's murderously slow. Like, still at only one percent after five minutes slow.

"Won't they suspect if we're on the VPN for hours sending stuff?" I ask.

"No. It'll look like someone left their computer on. And it'll pick up here in—Ah."

The download jumps suddenly to five percent. And keeps jumping in small but steady increments.

My lungs release. Oh God, that was stressful. I'm going to spend an hour or so staring at this download window, worrying and giving myself a headache.

Finn rises, grabs the back of my chair, and wheels me over to an empty desk. "Wait here. It's time for the entertainment."

As I watch, he pulls open the desk drawer and takes out a Go board. It's a simple one, the kind you'd give someone just learning the game, nothing like the elegant one he has at home.

But the beauty of Go is its simplicity. We could play as easily with some rocks and a grid scratched out in the dirt.

Finn sets the board down. "White or black?"

It feels like he's asking me something more momentous, something that will reverberate through my life. Black goes first, which would give me the advantage… but I don't need any kind of advantage over him.

"White," I say and not because I want to beat him from the disadvantaged position. I only want to… to play with him. To be with him.

Finn takes the bag of black stones and hands me the white. He makes his first move almost carelessly. "I've been thinking about some stuff."

"Oh?" I try to focus on the board, on thinking through some kind of strategy, but my heart is pounding too loudly. "Like what?"

I make my move, hardly even noticing where I've put the marker. So much for strategy.

"About how you and I work well together." He sets his stone right next to mine, white nestled against black. As far as strategy goes, it makes no sense. But my mouth is suddenly dry.

I slowly set another marker down, next to his first one. Again, there's zero strategy behind it. "I thought hackers were lone wolves?"

He puts his marker next to mine again. We're making a very pretty pattern here, but it's not much of a game. "Right," he says, looking at what he's done. "Because Anonymous is just one person."

I think I understand what he's getting at. I understand so much that my nerves are running riot. Just to be sure, I put another white stone on the board. Again, right next to his. "But you're a lone wolf."

He doesn't make his next play. Instead, he stares at the board, at the alternating white-and-black pattern we've put there, the dark and light intermingled, his expression bleak. "This is coming out all fucked up. None of this is what I meant to say."

My mouth is bone dry now, and my heart is knocking against my ribs. "What did you mean to say then?"

"I can't find any of the right words. Probably because I'm speaking with my heart."

He lifts his head, and his gaze is so raw my skin tingles.

This is so sappy. He doesn't do sappy and neither do I, but when he said *heart,* my own heart started to shimmy.

"So," I say slowly, letting the wild hope run free in my chest, "your heart isn't making any sense?"

His smile is slow and gorgeous. "That's the thing. It does make sense, except I can't put it into words. I want to be with you. I want to code together, live together, sleep together… do everything together. Like forever." He spreads his hands wide. "I love you. Completely and totally. That's what I mean to say."

I put my hand over my mouth, catching a happy scream. Instead of telling him I feel the same, I launch myself at him, scattering the game board as I do. He catches me easily, gathering all of me up.

Between kisses I keep saying, "I love you, I love you, I love you."

He's smiling and kissing me at the same time, and there's so much damn happiness between us I swear I can see it glowing.

"Do you remember," he asks, "when we were cracking into January's phone and you looked at me and asked if I even knew how to code? I was head over heels then, although I didn't know it."

"And you asked if I was for real. And I was head over heels too."

He grins at me. "So can we move your stuff to my place tomorrow?"

"I'm surprised you haven't already done it. You love to arrange things."

"I love to arrange things for you." He slips a hand under my shirt. "Among other things…"

The computer dings. I sit up so fast I almost smack into his chin. "The upload! We completely forgot it."

I dash over to the computer, Finn close behind me. I have to wake up the monitor, but when I do, my heart skips a beat.

Upload complete.

Finn quickly disconnects from the Corvus servers. It's kind of anticlimactic really, especially after Finn told me he loved me. And that he wanted me to move in. And spend the rest of his life with me.

"How will we know it worked?" I ask.

He takes my hand. I don't think I've ever felt anything so right in my life. "I think we'll know," he says. "Somehow."

I'm convinced he's correct.

CHAPTER 28

"Oh look." I spin around my laptop so that Doc can see the Fucked Company forums. "It looks like Corvus is shuttering an entire division. The rumor is it was hacked and a virus wiped everything out a few months ago."

Doc leans over in the bed and makes a clucking sound. "That's really too bad. I wonder who could've done that."

I take advantage of her closeness to kiss her nose. "Probably someone dangerously smart. Devastatingly handsome. And mind-blowingly good in bed."

She laughs, then gets serious. "Are we sure this is the Oracular division?"

"Well, the Oakland PD quietly canceled the panopticon last week. Shutting the division is probably a response to that."

Doc frowns. "Yeah, but the Gordian buildings are still going up."

We saw them today as we were moving Ray into his new apartment. The outcry over the *Disrupt Dispatch* article was pretty intense, which surprised me. I thought people didn't really care anymore, but I was wrong.

From there, it was pretty easy to get Ray a new trial, and I made sure to hire the great white sharks of the criminal-justice world—the apex predators who never lost a case. It took several months, but in the end, justice prevailed.

Ray was released from prison yesterday, and the happiness on Doc's face made all of it worth it and then some. He's still on his meds—for now—and we've moved him into an apartment in his old neighborhood so he can be close to his cats. I've got a team of home health aides who'll be with him twenty-four seven. His mental illness will probably never be cured, but this arrangement will give him a fighting chance. And once he's settled in, there's some math and coding stuff I want him to work on for me. It never hurts to have another math genius around.

"Do you think he'll be okay?" Doc asks.

"We're fifteen minutes away, the aide is there with him, and did you see how happy he was to see his cats? I think he'll be fine."

"I just don't think I can stop worrying about him."

"You don't have to. But you know I'm here to carry as much of that burden as I can."

She nuzzles my beard. "I know. And I love you for it. You're right. He'll probably be fine. And wasn't it nice that he got to see Kevin today too?"

Oh yeah, I also had to hire a team of sharks to get Kevin off and find an apartment for him. But someone needed to watch Ray's cats once Doc moved in with me.

All in all, everything's worked out perfectly. Oracular is dead, the panopticon is canceled, Ray is free, and Doc is here with me. Oh, and Corvus has been exposed as the frauds they are. They're not dead and buried, but they're definitely wounded.

Doc grabs the remote control from the nightstand. "Time for the local evening news."

"How can you watch that crap?" I grumble. "They never report on anything serious, just car crashes and robberies."

She shrugs. "It's a soothing ritual."

"You just want to ogle the weatherman."

She leers at me. "I love the way his butt wiggles when he predicts a heat wave."

That's it. I toss the covers off her and lower my mouth to her neck, kissing the soft skin there until she starts to giggle. "I'll show you a heat wave," I growl.

"What the…" She pushes at my head suddenly. "What is that?"

"We're so sorry," the anchor says, "but we're having trouble with the chyron tonight. We can't turn it off, and we can't change the text. Someone's hacked it."

I smile into her collarbone. I knew it would work.

"Dr. Ramona Blythe," Doc reads off the screen, "will you marry me?" She pinches my belly. "Finn, did you do this?"

I gasp in mock horror. "No, I didn't. Who's this other asshole who's proposing to you through the local news?"

She punches my arm, but she's laughing. "You can't just hack a system whenever you want something. You could have asked me like a normal person."

"Why not?" I nip at her throat and enjoy her shiver. "Hacking got me you."

She does her sigh, which goes straight to my cock. "Those poor anchors. You're driving them crazy."

I lift my head, search her expression. "What about you? Do I drive you crazy? Crazy enough to say yes?"

She loops her arms around my neck, pulling me down for a shattering kiss. "Yes, you drive me crazy." She lifts her hips, rubbing the center of herself against my cock. "And yes, I'll marry you."

So I set about driving her even crazier.

Raleigh fell in love with billionaire romance as a teenager thanks to Harlequin Presents. She fell in love with San Francisco in her twenties thanks to how charming the city was. And she fell for a coding genius thanks to how charming *he* was.

Naturally, she had to put all of the things she loved into her romances.

You can find her online at www.raleighdavis.com.

www.ingramcontent.com/pod-product-compliance
Lightning Source LLC
Chambersburg PA
CBHW050255110726

47898CB00007B/2421